Stowaway to the Mushroom Planet

By Eleanor Cameron

The Wonderful Flight to the Mushroom Planet

Stowaway to the Mushroom Planet

Stowaway to the Mushroom Planet

by Eleanor Cameron

Little, Brown and Company
Boston New York London

ISBN 0-316-12541-5
LCCN 56-8461

10 9 8 7

COM-MO

PRINTED IN THE UNITED STATES OF AMERICA

This book is for Colin Cameron, for Chuck Fabian (who is the real Chuck of the story), and for all those children everywhere who asked for more stories about the boys who made *The Wonderful Flight to the Mushroom Planet*.

Contents

PART ONE: The Arrival of Horatio

1	A Visitor out of the Night	3
2	A View of Basidium	11
3	Tyco Bass's Notebook	20
4	A Very, Very Clever Young Man	30
5	The Arrival of Horatio	37
6	Horatio Does Some Sleuthing	53
7	In the Dead of Night	60

PART TWO: The Stowaway

8	Farewell to Earth	69
9	Chuck and David's First Fight	79
10	Worse Than Nothingness	90
11	The Disappearance of Mebe and Oru	96
12	Escape from the Mushroom People	110
13	The Hall of the Ancient Ones	120

14   The Anger of the Ancient Ones   133
15   The Triumph of Horatio   143
16   In the Path of the Meteors   157
17   The Young Lady Named Bright   163

PART THREE: The Fall of Horatio

18   Hen-tracks   173
19   Horatio's Escape   182
20   The Return to Space   190
21   Pride Goeth . . .   196

PART ONE

The Arrival of Horatio

CHAPTER 1

A Visitor
out of the Night

To the very peculiar-looking little man trotting about in the dark trying to find Thallo Street, the sound of tapping came faintly. The neighborhood was quiet. Far off murmured the sea. Then, there it came again — *tap, tap* — *tap, tap, tap*. But he was far more intent upon finding Thallo Street, and a certain number on Thallo Street, than in wondering what that tapping could be.

If he had followed it down, he would have been led right to Mr. Tyco Bass's house — a house with a dome like a mushroom's and with a most mysterious-looking tube jutting out at one side through an opening in the dome. Under the dome was the smallest and most perfect little observatory in the world, and at the desk in there sat David and Chuck. David was pecking away at Mr. Bass's portable typewriter.

It was after dinner. Dr. and Mrs. Topman, David's father and mother, and Cap'n Tom Masterson, Chuck's grandfather, had given the boys permission to stay the night at Mr. Bass's all by themselves. They had made their own dinner: a can of beans heated up, pickles, fried eggs, bread and jam, and some rather melted ice cream. And they agreed it was the best dinner they'd ever had, cooked on Mr. Bass's stove, served on his dishes, and eaten in his living room where they were surrounded by his remarkable paintings of the planets.

It was now almost two months since David's and Chuck's good friend Tyco had taken off in such an unheard-of fashion, leaving his home and his tiny observatory with its excellent telescope, together with the rest of his property, entirely to the two boys. Already, the Society of Young Astronomers and Students of Space Travel had been formed, just as he had asked that it be, and had proved at once an enormous success.

Because David and Chuck had found the name of a certain Dr. Horace Frobisher many, many times in Tyco Bass's notebooks, they decided the two must have been the best of friends. Certainly it seemed likely, for Dr. Frobisher was a very famous astronomer at the San Julian Observatory in California, not far from Pacific Grove where the boys lived and where Mr. Bass had lived before his disappearance.

So it was that the boys were now writing the doctor a letter asking him to come and talk to their Society about space travel, or other planets, or the stars, or anything he liked. David's brown head and Chuck's dark one were bent over the table. There was silence while they considered. Then Chuck made a suggestion. The keys of the typewriter tapped again, and David's face grew red from having to write such an important letter without any mistakes.

"There!" he exclaimed at last, reading over what he had written with great pride. "Now you sign, Chuck."

And so Chuck did, holding the pen tightly and taking a deep breath, which he continued to hold while he signed. Then David took the pen, added his name, and out they went into the shadowy, silent streets to put their letter into the mailbox.

But no sooner had they turned the corner of Thallo Street, upon which Mr. Bass's house stood, than Chuck grasped David by the arm. Silently he pointed — and there, scurrying along the other side of the road, now dimly seen, now hidden again in darkness, was a small figure peering this way and that — stopping, retracing, hesitating — then hurrying on again.

"Is it a *man*?" whispered Chuck.

"Not tall enough," whispered back David.

"But it's — it's — he's got a *tall hat* on!"

So the little man had, and something that floated out behind him as he vanished under the trees into the garden of the house opposite.

"Let's follow!" said Chuck in a low, excited voice. And in a flash he had darted across the street with David at his heels.

Yet how queer! For when they got into that dark, rustling garden, there wasn't a soul to be seen. They followed every path, looked behind every bush and tree, even stole quietly — quietly — up onto the veranda of the house. But no one was there. Then suddenly David knew he was afraid, and so must Chuck have been, for as one boy they raced into the street again, ran as fast as they could to the nearest mailbox, and were back at Mr. Bass's before you could have blinked.

But no sooner were they in the house and about to go up to the observatory to have a look at Basidium, the Mushroom Planet, and perhaps at

6

the moon and Venus, than the knocker sounded —
tock! — *tock!* — *tock!* — on the front door, very loud
and clear and firm.

"Oh golly," groaned Chuck. "What'll we do,
Dave?"

"It's *him!*" said David in a low, sort of solemn
voice as though their fates were sealed. "I know
it is."

"Shall we answer?"

David hesitated. Because even if, like David,
you are so inquisitive that you will venture into the
most dangerous places, or, like Chuck, you are
short and solid and strong and an absolutely fear-
less fighter — still, it's a pretty scary thing to have
an appearing-disappearing stranger knock at your
door in the darkness.

Finally David said, "We've *got* to answer. All
the lights are on."

And so, reflecting that they should never, never
have been so foolish as to ask to stay here alone
all night, David led the way downstairs. But it
was Chuck who turned on the porch light, opened
the peephole in the door and applied an eye — and
then leaped back with a yelp. For an exceedingly
large brown eye was immediately applied on the
other side. David, overcome with a mixture of such

tense fear and violent curiosity that his stomach felt as if it were turning over, now took his turn. And how his chin dropped in astonishment!

For the brown eye having been politely withdrawn, David beheld in the light of the porch lantern the most outlandish little man imaginable. He was only a mite taller than the boys, *very* thin, and as though to add to his thinness he was dressed in an exceedingly tight old-fashioned suit. He had a worn and faded black cape flung about his shoulders, and a much-abused, ancient auto robe folded neatly over one arm. He had gloves on, shapeless gloves, badly in need of mending, as was the battered carpetbag he carried. On his large head he wore a rakishly tilted opera hat, and under that hat was a face so familiar that the very look of it brought an almost unbelieving joy to David's heart. The face had an alert, pointed expression as though the little man expected to see someone pop out from under a bush at any moment. But above all, this face was so like that of the boys' dear friend, Mr. Tyco Bass — the large eyes, the small, eager features, and the big head — that David let out a gasp of delight and threw the door open wide.

"Good evening," said the stranger in flutelike,

haunting tones. "I am Mr. Theodosius M. Bass, a cousin of Tyco Bass's. And this, I presume, is, at long last, 5 Thallo Street."

"Oh, Mr. Theodosius! Mr. Theodosius!"

How many, many times the two boys had talked about this wandering cousin of Mr. Bass's, spoken of his possible habits and personality, and about how it would feel to meet him. For he was the only other living member on earth of the race of Mushroom People, or Basidiumites, besides Mr. Tyco Bass, whom they had any inkling of at all. And now their Mr. Bass was gone to another planet.

"Come in — come in!" they cried, and introduced themselves at once.

Mr. Theodosius beamed at this warm welcome. His eyes shone with pleasure. Now he stepped briskly in and set down his carpetbag with the robe folded beside it. Next he removed his opera hat, the nap of which, once black and shiny, appeared now to be a rather dull greenish-brown with age and weathering. With a light tap on the top, he caused it to snap down as flat as a dinner plate, and after that he peeled off his shabby gloves as elegantly as though he were in the court of Queen Elizabeth. Then he looked all about, smiling

"My, my," he sighed, "how many years it has been since I have seen this house, with the round dome of Tyco's observatory making it look so pleasantly like a mushroom, and the tube of his telescope reaching up toward the skies! Do you know, I had completely forgotten where the house was! But Tyco? Is he at home? I am sure you can understand how I look forward to seeing him."

The two boys glanced at one another.

"We're so sorry, Mr. Theodosius," exclaimed Chuck. "But you're just too late. You see, Mr. Bass blew away."

Strangely enough, Mr. Theodosius showed no surprise at this seemingly impossible statement, but simply pushed out his lower lip and nodded gravely.

"Ah," he said. "Yes. I see. Well, it explains everything, then — that intense urge of mine to come to Pacific Grove as quickly as I could from clear on the other side of the world. I was camped with some Tibetans in Northern Mongolia when the word 'Tyco' came to me as clearly as though someone had cried it aloud on the night wind. But he blew away, you say. Yes — yes, that is pre-*cisely* what one would have expected of him."

CHAPTER 2

A View of Basidium

David and Chuck stared at one another, for that had always been their Mr. Bass's word — "precisely." There were so many things about Mr. Theodosius that reminded them of their old friend! Eagerly they ushered him into the living room where every piece of furniture, having been made especially for Mr. Bass, was slightly smaller than normal so that the boys always felt more comfortable here than anywhere else. The blinds were drawn, and the lamplight shone warmly on those pictures of the planets that Mr. Bass had painted. How cozy and homelike it all was!

Mr. Theodosius stood for a moment in silence looking all about, then he turned to them and his eyes gleamed.

"I wonder," he said, "I wonder if it is possible I could settle down after all these years — *here*, per-

11

haps. You see," he explained, sinking into Mr. Bass's chair as though it were quite natural for him to choose that one especially, "I have always been a wanderer, urged on by some mysterious need to find a place I could call my own. But such a place I have never found. I have been in every corner of the earth — some of my adventures you would scarcely believe — but still I can find no peace. Once I thought the Aleutians might be the answer — but oh, the cruel winds, the fogs, the bitter cold! A great *mist*-ake, you might say, eh?" And he darted the boys a sudden, twinkling glance, and they grinned at one another and knew with certainty they were going to get along with Mr. Theodosius.

"Something you'll never *fog*-et, you mean!" burst out Chuck, and then he slapped his knee and roared with laughter. David looked disgusted, but Mr. Theo seemed to think it a fine pun, and laughed and laughed. But then all at once he grew sober and cleared his throat.

"You know," he said, "no matter where I've been, I've always managed to get off a note to my cousin, Tyco. And occasionally, if I've stayed in one place long enough, I've heard from him in return. The last time I wrote, there was some little question of a project he had in mind — some question of inventing a lens filter, for a telescope, I believe, in order to make a certain astronomical discovery. Did he ever speak of it to you boys?"

David's heart stopped for a moment. Now there was a long, questioning pause, and then Chuck's and David's eyes met, and in the look they sent one another was the message that each boy knew in his bones that Mr. Theodosius was all right and that it was quite safe to tell him everything.

"Mr. Theodosius," began David, "Mr. Bass not only *told* us about this filter he invented, but we've seen how it works on his telescope. We've seen the discovery it made possible — a little planet only thirty-six miles in diameter. And we've not only looked through the telescope at it, but we've *been* there, all by ourselves, in a space ship!"

Following this staggering announcement, there was another silence in which David and Chuck watched with the hugest pleasure one expression after another take its way across Mr. Theo's face.

"You've *been* there, you say? In a space ship," he got out at last. "Well, really — I — goodness gracious! And here I thought *I* was a traveler. But now it seems to me that, by comparison, I've scarcely been anywhere. Tell me," he went on,

13

"tell me all about it — about the journey, what everything looked like, the emotions you felt."

And so, interrupting one another, correcting, reminding each other every now and then of half-forgotten incidents, Chuck and David poured out the almost unbelievable story of their wonderful flight to the Mushroom Planet . . .

"Called Basidium, you see, Mr. Theodosius," said David, "partly because it's covered with mushrooms — some much taller than we are — and partly because the people who live there are spore, or Mushroom People —"

"Who live in a kind of mist," broke in Chuck, "and a lucky thing for them, because if Basidium *weren't* surrounded by this sort of blue-green mist, very pale and winding and coming and going all the time, they'd be almost blinded by earth-light. You see, Basidium's only 50,000 miles out, so when you look up, the earth seems enormous."

"We made it there in two hours, of course," explained David in a matter-of-fact voice, "because we *had* to travel at 25,000 miles an hour in order to escape the earth's pull —"

"Or gravity," added Chuck.

"Ah," said Mr. Theodosius, blinking rapidly. "Yes. Quite so. I — WHAT? — *25,000 miles an hour,*

14

you say?" He swallowed and looked stricken, absolutely appalled. "I never heard of such a thing," he managed finally. "Tell me, what in the name of goodness gave you the courage to go in the first place? Did Tyco send you?"

"Yes," replied David, remembering as he spoke that tremendous, breath-taking moment when little Mr. Bass, sitting in the very chair where Mr. Theodosius sat now, had announced that he wished them to start at once, that very night, for the Mushroom Planet, a journey no other human being had ever taken. "You see, first of all he put an announcement in the newspaper for two boys to build a space ship. And so we did, Chuck and I, and brought it here to him. Then he told us that his people on Basidium were in danger, and that unless we went there and saved them immediately, they would die."

"And Ta, the king of the Mushroom People," broke in Chuck, "gave us a necklace of the most beautiful stones you've ever seen, to thank us for coming. We still have the necklace. We keep it upstairs now, along with Mr. Bass's filter, in his wall safe."

"Basidium!" breathed Mr. Theodosius. "How that name haunts me. Basidium, of course, means a form of spore-bearing organ having to do with basidiomycetous fungi —"

"And fungi are rusts and smuts and mushrooms," finished Chuck, knowing all this by heart long since.

"Yes — a perfect name for that little planet — a perfect name," exclaimed Mr. Theo, "for such a damp, cool, misty place as it must be. Tell me," he begged, "tell me, if you can, *exactly* what it is like."

And so the two boys tried to describe Basidium to him: how beautiful the earth-light was drifting through the pale green mists, how the space ship had looked like a greenish-silver arrow resting on the surface of Basidium, and what a queer feeling it had given them to see the horizon so curved and close on the little planet.

As they talked, Mr. Theodosius listened with absorbed attention.

"What language did you speak?" he asked.

"We can't remember," said Chuck sadly, "only that it was not our own. We can't get back even one word. We've tried and tried every way we can think of."

"A little cool, blue-green planet —" murmured Mr. Theo. "How I should love to see it!"

"But you can!" shouted David. "You can, Mr. Theodosius. Why didn't we think of it? All you have to do is look through Mr. Bass's telescope."

So now they all trooped up the flight of steep and narrow stairs that led to the observatory. And when Chuck opened the door and they stepped inside that small domed room, lined with books, fitted out with every instrument an explorer of the skies could possibly need, Mr. Theodosius heaved a sigh and a look came over his face of an adventurer who is on the verge of some final discovery. He went at once to the telescope and eagerly, impatiently, stared upward.

"Does the astronomical world know of Tyco's filter by now and of this new planet it has brought into sight?"

"Great jumping kadiddle fish, *no!*" exclaimed Chuck. "The news'd spread all over, and maybe a big space ship would be built, and Mr. Bass says human beings in large numbers and the little shy Mushroom People would never mix. We've promised him to keep all this a *dead, dark secret!*"

"I see," said Mr. Theo. He looked very thoughtful.

Now David opened the safe, took out a small,

round object of gl. ss to which was attached a long cord, and plugged the cord into a wall socket.

"Mr. Bass's marvelous Stroboscopic Polarizing Filter," he announced, fitting the filter firmly over the eyepiece of the telescope. "His own private invention that no one on earth knows about but Chuck and me and our folks, and now you, Tyco Bass's cousin."

"The filter's what allows us to see things that no other astronomers in the whole world can see, Mr. Theodosius," added Chuck with huge pride. "Just think of that! We can even see the surface of Venus, f'rinstance, through all its vapors; but best of all, we can see Basidium! Now, here's a chart of —"

"But *why* does this Stroboscopic Polarizing Filter allow you to see these things?" interrupted Mr. Bass in awed amazement.

"Well, we don't know exactly, except that a stroboscope interrupts light periodically, Mr. Bass said. And polarization —"

"Ah, yes," finished Mr. Theodosius, narrowing his eyes and tapping the side of his nose thoughtfully with one extremely long finger, "polarization affects light rays in such a way that they take definite paths — circular or straight or elliptical.

18

Amazing! Only Tyco would ever think of how to make the combination of the stroboscope and the polarizing process work. Now, *how*, do you suppose . . . ?"

"Oh, Mr. Bass just chuckled when we asked him *that!* O.K., Chuck, read out the positions, will you?"

Now David flipped a switch and the gentle hum of a tiny motor, like the sound of a hummingbird's wings, filled the room. David twirled certain knobs and dials at the base of the telescope and then the instrument swung slowly around and upward into position. While Chuck read from the chart the correct seasonal positions of Basidium, David squinted and peered and made several adjustments of the filter. Finally, "There!" he said, and Mr. Theodosius, almost fearfully, put his eye to the small glass disc. One hand, resting on the telescope, was trembling with excitement.

Now he gazed, and gazed, and gazed, as if he simply could not have enough of looking at Basidium. Then at last he spoke.

"Yes, there is no mistake," he murmured. "I must go at once. There is no question — absolutely none. In fact, we shall all three go."

CHAPTER 3

Tyco Bass's Notebook

"You don't mean . . . !" cried the boys.

"Indeed I do," replied Mr. Theodosius calmly. "To Basidium, by all means." Then with his face screwed up, his hands propped on his incredibly thin shanks, and his whole matchstick body bent tensely forward, he peered once more at the tiny planet. "You still have your space ship, I presume?"

"But that's just it," mourned David, "we haven't. It's gone — beaten to smithereens by the sea." And he felt, all over again, that awful hollow open in the pit of his stomach, just as it had when he stood on the bleak and lonely shore of Cap'n Tom's beach and knew that the beautiful ship he and Chuck had built so carefully and lovingly was gone forever. Chuck, too, looked fearfully cast-down, as though the memory of that time were almost too much to bear.

"Tut!" exclaimed Mr. Theodosius. "Dear, dear! I *am* sorry, boys. However" — and he waved one slim, elegant hand about — "it's really a small matter. You see, we shall just build a better one."

For a moment Chuck and David couldn't think of a word to say. *Build a better one!* And why not?

"But the rocket motor, Mr. Theodosius!" cried David.

"And the fuel tanks —" reminded Chuck.

"And the fuel —"

"And the sealer for the outside, so we won't be killed by the sun's rays —"

"And the oxygen urn — what about the oxygen urn, Mr. Theodosius? What about *that?* It went 'Pheep! Pheep!' all the way to Basidium and back."

"We'd have built another space ship ages ago," explained Chuck, "if only we could have managed somehow about all those things. We want to go back so much."

"You see, we want to be sure Mrs. Pennyfeather's all right. She's my hen, and we took her as a mascot, and left her there for the Basidiumites. But she might be lonely."

"So we thought we could take John, her husband, and all her children if we ever went again —"

"Besides, we want to see Ta, the king of the

Mushroom People. But, you know," David said, "even if there weren't Ta, or Mrs. Pennyfeather, or anybody, we'd still feel we had to go back. There was something about that whole journey . . ."

"The way the stars looked out in space — and the earth, when you looked back and saw it hanging there . . ."

Then both boys were silent, staring off, remembering, and they both shivered.

Mr. Theodosius watched their faces. He appeared to consider deeply; then a ghost of a smile played at the corner of his lips.

"Well, it just might be . . ." he said. "Oh, if only I had a hint or two! *Did* Tyco, by any chance, leave any writings?"

"*Leave any writings!* Look here!" And David turned to the wall safe and got out Mr. Bass's two notebooks, one entitled A Few Hitherto Undiscovered Facts Concerning the Satellite Basidium-X, and the other Random Jottings on Some Inventions of Tyco M. Bass. Then he brought forth Ta's necklace.

At the sight of it, Mr. Theo stretched out his hands, and with an exclamation of awe and wonderment held it up and turned it all about, now this way, now that. Over the satiny surface of the stones, viridian green, sulphur yellow, cinnabar red, and such hues as would be almost impossible to put a name to, the light played as over some jeweled serpent.

"I can't tell you what the sight of this necklace does to me," he said. "I have a feeling of being taken back — and back — a feeling of ancientness, as though centuries were passing in a flash. But at the same time, I have a feeling of the greatest happiness. It is all very, very strange."

"No," said David. "I don't think it's strange. I think it's natural. If Mr. Bass was a Mushroom Person, that means you are too, and that the Basidiumites are your people as well as his."

"A Mushroom Person," murmured Mr. Theo. "Quite so!"

Now he took up the Basidium notebook, and then, with a light in his eye, the RANDOM JOTTINGS. Eagerly he flipped over the pages, studying with intense interest Mr. Bass's scratchings. But David and Chuck, peering over his shoulder, lost hope all over again at the sight of them. Who on earth could make head or tail of those minute pothooks, like nothing so much as the trail a delirious and inky ant might leave in its progress across the page? But Mr. Theo was enormously excited.

"Good heavens, who would have dreamed . . ." he muttered. "But yes, yes, of course! I can only ask myself why this has never occurred to me. Brilliant! Positively brilliant! Ah, Tyco . . ." And the little man whipped back and forth among the pages with widening eyes as though he simply could not believe what he saw.

"But *tell* us!" begged David, hopping up and down, first on one foot and then on the other. "What does it say there?" And Chuck was so beside himself with impatience that he could only shake Mr. Theo's arm and bark, *"What? What?"*

Mr. Theo looked up with glazed eyes.

"I don't know how I am to make this clear to you. No, I cannot take the time now. I would have to begin too far back."

"But, Mr. Theodosius," protested David, "how can *you* understand what is written there? Are you an inventor and astronomer, as well as an explorer?"

"An astronomer, no," he replied. "At least not any more of an astronomer than I would have to be to use the stars for a guide when I've been lost in wild and trackless places for weeks at a time. As for being an inventor — well" — and here he laughed and shook his head as at the memory of something ridiculous — "there have been any number of times when I've been *forced* to be one. Oh, I could tell you of some ex-*tremely* tight moments when it was really a matter of life and death as to whether or not I could put together some outlandish contraption. But now" — and here Mr. Theodosius got up suddenly and, clasping his hands together, looked quite serious, "the cellar is what I must see next. I seem to recall that that was where Tyco worked."

So down they went. And Chuck turned on the cool, silver bubbles of light which Mr. Bass had invented and, muttering and exclaiming to himself in the most comical fashion, Mr. Theodosius darted from one strange-looking object to another.

"I declare!" the boys heard him cry. "Speaking of outlandish contraptions . . . !"

Then he went over to Mr. Bass's workbench, snatched open drawers, ran a prying, curious finger over the array of labeled bottles, picked up tools (most of which hardware dealers have never seen even in their wildest dreams), examined them closely, then turned at last and beamed at the two boys.

"Yes, it all comes back to me," he said. "It is all

just as I remember. My cousin, Tyco, was a *most* remarkable man. What joy it will be to follow along in his footsteps, working according to his directions!"

"But, Mr. Theo — I don't understand," exclaimed David, greatly puzzled. "Mr. Bass was always saying how he could never seem to get his inventions down on paper —"

"Which was why," went on Chuck, "none of them could ever be made by the big companies. He said his inventions were like certain shades of paint: he could never remember afterwards just how he got them."

Mr. Theo put back his head and laughed aloud.

"You know," he said, "if Tyco gave you the idea he was absent-minded, that must have been his little joke. I suppose he wasn't interested in getting some of his inventions onto paper; they just amused him. But I have never known a more careful person in all my life. Did he forget to think of the smallest detail that would be necessary for you to make a successful journey to Basidium and back? I believe not. If scientists were absent-minded —"

"We'd all be dead," finished Chuck.

"Pre-*cise*ly!" smiled Mr. Theo. "And as for these RANDOM JOTTINGS of Tyco's, they're about as random as the multiplication table. (Random means haphazard, you know, or accidental.) Everything Tyco has put down here is worked out with the greatest care. Of course, I'm sure no one else could read all this — no one but another Mushroom Person, that is. Our minds work in the same way."

Now Mr. Theo came over to them and put his arms around their shoulders — and there it was, the same feeling of mingled happiness and excitement they remembered when they were with Mr. Tyco Bass. It was as if an electric current had been turned on, low and steady and strong, so that life was completely changed somehow now that Mr. Theo had come.

All at once David noticed by the clock on the wall that it was nearly ten. As this was the beginning of summer vacation, the boys were being allowed late hours now and then, but they had promised, if they were to spend the night at Mr. Bass's, that they would be in bed by ten on the dot.

"Mr. Theo," said David, "Chuck and I will sleep on the two couches in the living room, so that you can have Mr. Bass's room. And if you stay, that will be your room for good. *Will* you stay?"

Mr. Theo smiled down at them, his small face with its great dark eyes lighting up all over.

"I am your friend, just as Tyco was, and I accept your hospitality most gladly. I shall be very happy to stay here. But I won't be going to bed just yet, because I have so much work to do. I couldn't *possibly* get to sleep until I have thoroughly studied this notebook of Tyco's on his inventions. Surely here, in his curious shorthand, I shall find the secret of every possible necessity for the space ship.

"As for you boys, you must set to work at once, early tomorrow morning, to build another space ship. Do you think you can do it?"

There wasn't a doubt of it, at least with Mr. Theo's help!

But all at once Chuck made a face as though something had hit him.

"Crikey! What about Dr. Frobisher? The next meeting of our Young Astronomers and Students of Space Travel is only five days away. What if he comes *then?*"

"You see," said David to Mr. Theo, "Dr. Frobisher was a good friend of Mr. Bass's. He's an astronomer up at the San Julian Observatory, and we thought maybe he'd like to come and talk to our Society, so we wrote him a letter. But what if he answers and says he can come right away?"

"Oh well," said Chuck airily, "we'll just have the

meeting, and then set off that very night for Basidium. It'll make a nice busy evening, that's all!"

"It will indeed," chuckled Mr. Theo, going over to the work bench and winding his long, spindly legs around Mr. Bass's stool as he settled himself with the notebook. "And we shall be ready to leave at the right time, I promise you. When I set my mind to a thing, it is done!"

CHAPTER 4

A Very, Very Clever
Young Man

On a sunny morning two days later, in a little town not far from the San Julian Observatory, a letter was dropped into the mailbox at 23 Amadon Street. It was the boys' letter and this was Dr. Frobisher's house. But it was certainly not the good doctor who now came to the door. *He* would have stood squinting up at the sparkling blue sky for a little, out of pure pleasure, before opening the mailbox. Then he would have ambled over to his roses just to see how they were coming along, and then picked one and put it in his buttonhole.

But not *this* young man! Good heavens, no! He hadn't even a second for such pointless nonsense — for *he* was Horatio Q. Peabody, the doctor's secretary. He had been given the key to the house while the Frobishers were away on vacation, and had come to get on with the typing of a manuscript, the doctor's new book, *A Study of the Interpenetrating Effects of Gravitational Fields upon the Orbits of Heavenly Bodies, upon the Speeds of Their Rotations As Well As upon Their Advances and Variable Deviations in a Space-Time Continuum.* A most important, difficult and impressive paper, as anyone can see with half an eye!

Also, Horatio had the mail to answer.

He was a tense, lean young man, very nervous, with bitten nails. "You really should try to relax and stop biting your nails, Horatio," Mrs. Frobisher was always reminding him, but he could never seem to remember. He was always bent on getting something done, and hated interruptions. He typed furiously — it was exhausting to hear him. But Dr. Frobisher considered him brilliant, a young man of great promise — but a little conceited, Mrs. Frobisher was afraid.

Now Horatio went inside, slammed the door, threw all the ads in the wastepaper basket, and ripped open the boys' envelope with one whip of his finger. He read:

DEAR DR. FROBISHER:

Some weeks ago Mr. Tyco Bass, the noted astronomer, went off on a long journey and left all his property to us. According to his wishes his house is now a Society for Young Astronomers and Students of Space Travel. The Society has been formed and we would like you to come at your earliest convenience and talk to us about whatever you like. You will be our first lecturer, and we know this would please Mr. Bass. We see by his notebooks that you were his friend.

Our next meeting will be on the evening of June the 30th. Please let us know right away if you can come.

Yours respectfully,
CHARLES MASTERSON
DAVID TOPMAN

Horatio Q. Peabody frowned. The letter annoyed him, though he wasn't sure why. He couldn't make up his mind whether the writers were too young to be bothered with, or just peculiar. But then, he thought, even college men these days have no idea of how to write a good letter. That "Students of Space Travel" he did not like at all. Any talk of flying saucers or of space ships disgusted him. To his amazement, Dr. Frobisher seemed actually to enjoy discussions of space travel — great man that he was! This, Horatio could not understand. To him, such talk was twaddle and quite beneath the notice of famous scientists.

All the same, Horatio said to himself, this request just *might* be made to lead to some very interesting results. He remembered a letter from this Mr. Tyco Bass to Dr. Frobisher that spoke of some "astounding discovery" which Mr. Bass was about to make. The doctor had chuckled at the time, for Mr. Bass was always working on astounding discoveries. Still, there had been a note of seriousness about that letter which had given Dr. Frobisher pause to think. And perhaps, reflected Horatio, Mr. Bass really had been on the brink of something that would upset the whole astronomical world, for Dr. Frobisher had regarded him as being no ordinary person.

Horatio sat in the warm morning sun thinking hard. What if *he*, Horatio Q. Peabody, could get hold of whatever secret it was Tyco Bass had been working on? Why, then — then, at last, he could make a reputation for himself. Then he, too, like Dr. Frobisher, could become a Very Important Person. For there was nothing, absolutely nothing in the whole world, Horatio wanted more than to become a Very Important Person.

Now Horatio breathed a little faster. Of course this letter from Pacific Grove happened to be written to the doctor. If it were sent on to him at his hotel, he could easily drive to Pacific Grove from San Francisco. Still, said Horatio to himself, why should the doctor trouble about these amateurs? It would hardly be worth his time. Then, too, he — Horatio Peabody — had always dreamed of giving a lecture before a large gathering. But he had never been asked, and it was always Dr. Frobisher this, that, and the other, so that Horatio was lost in the great man's shadow. Nobody ever noticed him or asked his opinion when Dr. Frobisher was around.

Now Horatio's eyes suddenly narrowed. He bit off what spare thumb nail he had and was about to go to work on the other when he made up his mind in a flash. He whipped a sheet of paper into the typewriter and rattled off the following reply:

SAN JULIAN, CALIFORNIA

GENTLEMEN:

Unfortunately, Dr. Frobisher is away on a vacation at this time. In the meanwhile, I am handling his affairs. Though I am extremely busy on a piece of astronomical research, I shall be happy to give the lecture in his place if your Society so desires. I happen to believe that everyone, even though they be amateurs in astronomy, should be encouraged in the exploration of this humbling and awe-inspiring science. Also, you seem anxious to get hold of a person of sound reputation.

Therefore, I shall arrive on the afternoon train in Monterey in good time to give the lecture on the evening of June 30 — unless otherwise advised. My fee would usually be $100 per lecture, plus traveling expenses. But as a special favor to your Society, which is a new one, I shall simply charge for the expense of the journey.

> I remain, most cordially,
> HORATIO QUIMBY PEABODY

Horatio signed his letter with large flourishes to the tails of the "y's" and sealed it up, deeply pleased with himself. He often spent time in signing his name with a flourish, for he liked his name.

Next he went over and looked at himself in the mirror: a sandy young man with freckles and bristling hair and quick, beady eyes. How he admired that alert glance of his! He had often practiced glancing in the mirror, as well as lecturing before large, learned bodies. Already he heard himself speaking — Professor Peabody, or Dr. Peabody, perhaps. Now he began outlining in his mind what he would say.

He smiled to himself. Inside of another week, what new path might not open before him? Who could tell what turn of fate lay hidden?

CHAPTER 5

The Arrival of Horatio

By the morning of the following Saturday, the day on which Horatio Q. Peabody was to arrive, the boys had almost finished the space ship and were now busily putting on the finishing touches.

They were down in the cave on Cap'n Tom's beach. The space ship, long and smooth and cigar-shaped, just as the first ship had been, rested firmly on its four-wheeled carrier-base. And just like the first ship, this one, too, had a fine, strong, four-bladed tail, level on the ends, and built at right angles around the rocket exhaust. Over its whole length it was covered with strips of aluminum sheeting, which shone like some precious metal in the reflection of the brilliant sun outside the cave's mouth. Inside the cave it was cool and damp, and the space ship seemed to light it as though by some mysterious radiation of its own. Outside, the waves flashed as they curved over and pounded on the hard, white

37

sand. Gulls were being blown about the vast, windy reaches of the dazzling sky.

"What a day!" exclaimed Chuck. He stood at the mouth of the cave and watched a perfect V of black, long-necked cormorants skim low over the surface of the water. "This means it'll be a swell, clear night to take off for Basidium." Then he turned. "Just think, Dave — *tonight's the night*."

"Yep," said David. How many times during the past week he'd awakened in the dark to lie there wondering if he could possibly wait for that moment of take-off to arrive. Now it was almost here.

Once more they went on with the work of putting in the big sheet of plastiglass which was to be the wide front window. The boys had just finished cutting the sheet a little larger than the window opening. Now they carefully lifted it up, placed it over the opening, and bolted it firmly down all around over an airtight rubber sealer. Then they cut strips of metal with their snippers and fastened them down over the edge of the plastiglass so as to make a neat frame.

"Boy, what a beautiful job!" sighed Chuck proudly, stepping back and taking a good, long look at their handiwork.

"And you did an especially good job on that bolt for the door," admitted David with great generosity, for he himself wasn't nearly so clever at working with his hands as Chuck was, and sometimes this made him a little unhappy.

"Isn't it funny," mused Chuck, "how everything's gone along like a dream. We always just *know* what to do, exactly the way we did before. O' course, we've taken five days this time, instead of three, but then this ship's bigger and we had to hunt hard for more old boat-ribs to make the frame. Lucky Cap'n Tom's friend had enough."

"Yes," said David in a low voice, "*just* enough. And lucky, too, about our being able to get those strips of aluminum from the war-surplus store. Or *was* it luck?"

"What do you mean, Dave?" Chuck shot him a queer little glance.

"Well, *you* know — and the way our fingers seemed to have an idea what to do all by themselves. Maybe Mr. Bass wants us to go to Basidium again — maybe he's helping us."

Chuck ran his hand over the beautifully curved surface of the space ship.

"Maybe!" he said. "Maybe! What do we do next, Dave?"

"Nothing. It's up to Mr. Theo now. Everything's in his hands."

Mr. Theodosius had fulfilled his tasks with the greatest eagerness and enthusiasm. He had even stored away emergency fuel tanks, filled and ready to be used, and there they were — piled up like big bullets at the back of the cave. Only the mechanism for turning the ship into free fall, so that it could land safely on its tail when it reached Basidium, and then again on its return journey to earth, remained to be finished. And on it, at this very moment, Mr. Theodosius was working feverishly.

That afternoon after lunch, Dr. Topman, David's dad, drove the boys into Monterey to meet the train. But when no elderly, learned-looking man got off, and the train drew away, they were horribly disappointed. What could have happened to Horatio Q. Peabody?

"Pardon me," barked a thin young fellow, striding up with a suitcase in one hand, a mashed felt hat in the other, and his string tie all on one side, "could you people tell me anything about a meeting of astronomers to be held at Pacific Grove tonight? I had supposed their society would send

40

one of the trustees to meet me, but I am afraid they have not thought it worthwhile. I really cannot understand it."

David and Chuck stared. This could not possibly be Professor Peabody! How their hearts sank!

"We're — *we're* the trustees," was all David could manage. And so feeble was his voice, and so startled and appalled was the sudden expression on the thin young man's face, that Dr. Topman couldn't help bursting into laughter.

"How do you do, Professor Peabody? I'm Dr. Topman," he said, holding out his hand. And Horatio took it, utterly unable to correct that title of "professor," to which he was not entitled at all, but which fell so richly on his ears. "This is my boy, David," Dr. Topman went on, "and this is Chuck Masterson, his friend. We're very glad to see you. I have my car right over here."

Horatio went cold with disappointment. Now the tone of that letter he'd received was explained. There *was* no society of earnest adults for whom he'd prepared his lecture — nothing, likely, but a bunch of noisy Cub Scouts bent on getting to the moon. Now he would have to rewrite everything he'd labored over so hard into a pep talk for infants. He was absolutely disgusted.

41

But in the car he cheered up a little.

"There's going to be an awfully big meeting tonight, Professor Peabody," said David, turning around eagerly in the front seat so that he could see the young man better.

"Local digniaries, 'n' everything," added Chuck, who was sitting in the back seat by Horatio with his feet on Horatio's suitcase.

"*Dignitaries*, y'mean!" shouted David.

"O.K., O.K.!" shouted back Chuck. "So you don't even know how to spell con-ve-ni-ence. C-o-n-v-i —"

"We invited several of them," said Dr. Topman in his firm, kindly voice, "as we thought this would be a rather special meeting. And we also asked over some of the students and professors from the College of the Peninsula. We hope you don't mind —"

"Mind!" exclaimed Horatio, going hot all over with enthusiasm and relief. Then he hastily controlled himself. "That is," he added in a more dignified way, "not at all — not at all." But what balm to his wounded pride were those words, "local dignitaries" and "students and professors from the College of the Peninsula." What a night this would be! Then he reflected shrewdly that, young as David and Chuck were, all the easier would prove the

42

important job of prying out of them the mystery of Tyco Bass's "astounding possibility."

Yes, yes! How neatly everything was playing into his hands.

At 5 Thallo Street, Dr. Topman let the boys and Horatio out of the car, and then drove away to make a call. But how strange, thought David, for he didn't feel a bit excited about showing Professor Peabody Mr. Bass's house. No, there was something about this young man that made him uncomfortable, and he couldn't imagine what it was. However, Chuck ran on ahead, ushered their visitor into the house very politely, and soon the two boys were pointing out Mr. Bass's paintings. They showed him the cozy little bedroom, the small kitchen "as neat and snug as a ship's galley," as Cap'n Tom had put it, and led him up the steep stairs to the observatory.

Horatio quivered. His eyes lighted on the little wall safe.

"And that?" he inquired lightly. "My, what an exceptionally good idea!"

"That's where we and Mr. Bass keep our most private possessions," declared Chuck proudly. "Things like —" But David gave him such a sharp poke in the ribs that Chuck grunted and was silent. Horatio took this all in, and his mind went bounding and panting ahead when he thought of the secrets that safe must hold.

"You know," he said pleasantly, "Dr. Frobisher was one of Tyco Bass's closest friends. There was nothing the two didn't confide in each other about their work. Among the most interesting projects, I thought, was the one Mr. Bass was working on — just before he left, I suppose it was. I am, as I told you, Dr. Frobisher's assistant, and we often discussed Tyco Bass. Of course, that last project of his was quite complicated, so I imagine it was a little beyond your understanding."

But then, to Horatio's surprise and indignation, the two boys suddenly became red in the face, and Chucky burst into loud guffaws of laughter, while David only just managed not to.

"Well, I'm afraid I really don't know what I've done to cause this," said Horatio huffily.

"Please excuse us, Professor Peabody," gasped David. "We didn't mean to laugh. But, it was — oh, I guess it was you saying Mr. Bass's discovery was *interesting*. It was that word that made us laugh — it just doesn't hitch, it's so tame. We're awfully sorry."

Ah, thought Horatio, so then this business of Tyco Bass's went *beyond* being a possibility and became an actual discovery. And he felt a sharp burst of triumph rise inside him, for already he had hit on something definite.

"Quite all right," returned Horatio kindly, with a large, beaming smile. "Let us say breath-taking, then, shall we? Yes, I think that's a much better word, don't you?"

But the boys did not reply. David glanced at Chuck, and that glance said, *Do Frobisher and Peabody know something — and if they do, how much do they know?* Surely Mr. Bass had not told, for he had said that the whole subject of Basidium must be kept a dead secret.

Meanwhile, Horatio was gazing all around with awe and respect.

"My, my," he murmured, "what a privilege it would be to work here — how exciting it would be. I feel the spirit of a great mind in the very air I breathe." Then he turned suddenly. "Or perhaps *fantastic* would be a better word still," he shot at them. "A far better word than breath-taking, eh?"

"Well, of course," said David offhandedly, "most of his discoveries were both."

"But this last one the most fantastic of all," persisted Horatio.

"What do *you* think?" inquired Chuck, grinning at Horatio in the most maddening fashion. "Why fantastic? In the way it will affect astronomy, do you mean?" he asked with slyness.

"Absolutely revolutionary!" cried Horatio. "Any astronomer will agree to that."

David drew in his breath.

"But have you and Dr. Frobisher *told* the other astronomers, then?" he exclaimed in alarm.

"Great Scott, no! But between ourselves we have agreed that the whole future of astronomy will be changed."

David's heart sank. For it sounded as if Dr. Frobisher and this Horatio Peabody *did* know something — maybe everything!

"We wouldn't know how it will be changed," he answered, unable to hide his anxiety and not certain now of just what it was safe to say. "I guess Chuck and I really don't understand much about it after all."

Now Horatio felt himself warm to his subject, for he saw clearly that David was feeling defeated and that he was very, very near to having a full confession.

"Why," he said, making a large gesture, "naturally we know that our ideas of the *solar* system can't change — that's been thoroughly explored — but when you get out beyond our galaxy —" and then he saw at once that he'd made a mistake, that he'd gone off on the wrong track entirely. Confound it! For the worry had vanished from the boys' eyes and they were both looking relaxed and merry.

But what had he said? *That the solar system had been thoroughly explored.* So! Then Tyco Bass's discovery had something to do with the sun and its nine planets and *not* with those suns out beyond it, or even beyond our galaxy. He turned away, his eyes cold as little pebbles, and glanced furtively at the safe. Chuck and David, he felt, were beaming with relief and this infuriated him. Somehow he had to get back on the track again. But now the boys seemed to feel it was time to go.

"Hear those noises down in the cellar, Professor Peabody?" remarked David, turning to him. "That's Mr. Theodosius Bass, Tyco Bass's cousin. He's staying here. He's just about as marvelous an inventor as Mr. Bass was, so maybe you'd like to meet him."

Horatio knew perfectly well that if he tried to find excuses to stay in the observatory any longer, it would only arouse the boys' suspicions. So he covered his annoyance with a pursed-up little smile, being far too irked to manage a big one. And at least,

47

he thought, clambering down the steep narrow stairs behind Chuck, he'd taken two steps in the right direction:

One, Tyco Bass had really discovered something.

Two, the discovery concerned some object within the solar system.

Down they went into the cellar, and as Mr. Theodosius was introduced to Horatio, David saw him glance at the young man with sharp, quick glances.

As for Horatio, he was dumbfounded at the sight of this queer-looking little man — his clothing, his body, his face, the size of his head, his large, clear, liquid-brown eyes.

"I had no idea Tyco Bass had a cousin," he managed to get out.

"I have been traveling," murmured Mr. Theodosius, "and am stopping off for a little. However, I expect to continue my travels shortly."

At this, Chuck snickered, and was punched.

Now Horatio turned to the glowing bubbles of light that illumined the basement, like no electric lights ever seen on earth. His eyes widened, and they widened still more as he stared about at the weird-looking contrivances littering the cellar floor and the crowded shelves.

On the workbench stood the mechanism for turning the ship around in space, but to look at it, one could not have told what it was. It looked somewhat like a gyroscope, but not exactly, and Chuck and David had named it the "auto-reversitron," because it reversed the ship all by itself. But not only did this remarkable instrument accomplish the turning of the ship: it also cut off the rocket motor, at the same time, so that when the ship was speeding tail-first toward Basidium (or toward earth, as the case might be) it would be in free fall. It would be sailing through space under the power which the rocket motor had given it. Only when it neared Basidium, or earth, would the motor be turned on again to keep the ship from crashing, from answering too violently the pull of gravity.

Horatio eyed the shining little object with its central orb and its enormous numbers of gears and its horizontal and vertical axes. "An invention of yours?" he inquired pleasantly of Mr. Theo.

"Oh, just a simple form of automatic pilot," replied Mr. Theo lightly. "It's just about finished — but I imagine it'll never be of any practical value to industry."

"Mr. Bass must have been a very, very busy man," observed Horatio. "I should like so much to have some of his inventions explained to me."

"My cousin," returned Mr. Theo, raising an eyebrow, "was a most *remarkable* man. And as I look over his notes which he left to us, I become more and more astounded at the range of his busy mind. I feel sometimes as if — yes, as if I'm plunging through a hole in space."

At mention of Mr. Bass's notes, Horatio's eyes had gleamed suddenly, but quickly he'd lowered his gaze away from Mr. Theodosius. Now he burst into a scornful laugh.

"A hole in space!" he cried in amazement. "What a preposterous thing for a man of science to say."

"Yes," said Mr. Theo, "perhaps it is, and yet I believe that there is almost nothing in the heavens nor on the earth which is too preposterous to be possible."

Horatio frowned. I'll bet he thinks Mr. Theo is loony, thought David. But that's fine — the loonier he thinks him, the better.

"I wonder," went on Horatio, looking very dignified and above any such childish nonsense as holes in space, "if you would tell me what the M stands for in Tyco Bass's name. I've always been rather curious about that."

"Certainly," replied Mr. Theo. "It stands for Mycetes. All of Tyco's and my people have had

that for a middle name. It is my own, of course —
Theodosius M. Bass, you see. It's a custom."

Horatio looked puzzled.

"A custom," he repeated. "Of your family, you
mean?"

"Of my race," said Mr. Theo.

There was a small silence while Horatio appeared
to take this in and to chew on it for a moment —
to no avail. Then when Mr. Theo begged to be ex-
cused so that he might get on with his work, Horatio gave a stiff little bow. Behind his back, David
turned and winked at Mr. Theo.

Upstairs, Horatio snapped his fingers.

"Mycetes!" he cried. "Of course! That means
fungus. You combine other words with it. But what
a *peculiar* middle name."

"Oh no," said Chuck matter-of-factly, "not a bit
peculiar, seeing as how it has to do with the Basses.
It's perfectly natural. They're Mushroom People,
you see."

Horatio Q. Peabody looked staggered. *"Mushroom People!"* he breathed. He opened his mouth
— and then closed it again. Now he seemed to con-
centrate deeply for a second or two, then to make
up his mind to something.

"You say Mr. Theodosius now occupies his cousin's former bedroom?" he asked, wandering with restless steps about the tiny living room.

"Yes, Professor Peabody. Chuck and I sometimes sleep here, on these couches, when our folks let us stay overnight as a special treat."

"Ah!" said Horatio. "Yes. Well, now, I've been wondering. This house fascinates me. So does Mr. Theodosius, as a matter of fact. Do you suppose, if I were very quiet, and no trouble at all, I might just curl up here on this couch for the night instead of putting your good mother to the inconvenience of having me there? All these books, for instance — when again shall I have the chance of exploring such a library? Tonight, after the lecture, I should so like to come here and read to my heart's content. Do you suppose, as a special favor, I might be allowed that privilege?"

David frowned and glanced at Chuck, and as before, a silent question seemed to travel between them. Then Chuck nodded.

"We-e-ll," said David. "O.K., Professor Peabody. I don't see why not. In fact, it might be the best idea after all."

CHAPTER 6

Horatio Does
Some Sleuthing

At the meeting that night, Horatio went to all kinds of trouble to make the lecture exciting. He had drawn enormous colored charts of the different planets to enchant the eyes of the children, and had entirely rewritten his talk so that he might watch the boys' expressions to find what they would tell him.

Instead of "Analysis of Sunspot Faculae as Revealed by Spectroheliographic Investigation," he had changed his subject to "Is There Life on Other Planets?" and he noticed shrewdly how the eyes of the boys shone with eagerness to hear what he would have to say.

First Horatio took the planets one by one and told of the terrible conditions that existed on each (terrible, that is, for human life): the melting heat of Mercury on the side of it where the sun never sets and the deathly frigidity on the other where it never rises, the ice-encrusted surface of Jupiter, the barrenness of Mars.

"It is nonsense," exclaimed Horatio, "to regard the canals of Mars other than as illusions, for each astronomer differs in his report of what he sees. Those canals, if they exist at all, are simply the results of seasonal changes and have nothing to do, I assure you, with farming Martians."

"Yes, but what about Venus?" piped up a girl's voice from the back of the room. "I betcha we could live there. I've been reading about Venus and it said nobody knows what kind of atmosphere there is under all those clouds that we can't see through. It said nobody has ever proved there's no oxygen or water *underneath* the cloud layer, and that maybe, for all we know, there are swamps on Venus like there were on earth millions of years ago, and the same kind of prehistoric animal and vegetable life. Maybe, if we went there, we'd find dinosaurs!"

"Gee whiz!" whispered Chuck gruffly into David's ear. "Why do girls always think they know so much?"

"Well, *some* of 'em know *something*," whispered back David. "You've got to admit *that*, anyway!"

Meanwhile Horatio Q. Peabody was smiling patiently.

"It is true, my dear young lady," he said with great kindliness, "that there may be dinosaurs on Venus. But it is my firm belief, I am sorry to say, that we shall never be able to prove it, for the simple reason that we shall never be able to get there."

And now, ignoring the bitterly disappointed faces of most of his young listeners, Horatio went on to tell of the fearful difficulties of space travel. He told why no space ship could exist in the heat that friction would create against the ship's sides as it rushed through the earth's atmosphere. He stated that men would go mad once they were released into the terrifying reaches of outer nothingness. And he explained in awful detail why a traveler would be crushed to jelly by the weight which unthinkable speed would press against his frail body.

"No, my friends," he finished, laughing and rubbing his hands together, "I am afraid we have been dreaming, with all our talk of space travel. It is really childish to speak of it — ah, that is —" and he looked somewhat embarrassed — "let us say it is extreme foolishness."

Now, last of all, he invited questions from the

55

audience, and Chuck, bursting with some mysterious joy, waved his hand violently.

"What about life on planetoids, Professor Peabody?" he cried. "What about that?" And his eyes sparkled with mischief, though Horatio could not imagine why. The question seemed to him to be simply silly.

"Planetoids," observed Horatio, looking pained, but still pleasant, "are, as we know, tiny planets, sometimes no more than a few miles in diameter —"

"Sometimes only thirty, or thirty-five miles in diameter," exploded Chuck.

"Correct. Therefore," went on Horatio, eying Chuck closely, "life on them is an even more fantastic and ridiculous idea than life on other planets, as planetoids are mere rocky missiles hurtling through space. They have no atmosphere at all, and no water, and therefore there is no way in which life could find even a foothold.

"Of course," continued Horatio, and now his eyes went to David's face and rested upon it, "how nice it would be if there were only some little world conveniently close by where we could explore the results of life developing differently than ours has done. Some place, it ought to be, which we could reach quickly, and where we might have the delight of seeing what path evolution has taken under conditions only a little different from our own. Strange plants — strange beings, smaller, perhaps, than we are, for who knows . . ."

Then Horatio stopped suddenly for the merest fraction of a second. *Strange beings, smaller, perhaps, than we are . . . !* And the person of Mr. Theodosius, no bigger than a boy of nine or ten, flashed across his mind's eye. Little Mr. Theodosius M. Bass, a member of the race of Mushroom People, David had said!

Yet in that fraction of a second Horatio's expression did not change. Now he put back his head and laughed. "But a mere pipe dream!" he cried.

And then, lo and behold, even as he said the words "pipe dream," he saw from his position above the audience that Chuck and David glanced quickly at one another with sparkling eyes. They nudged each other and seemed to hold their own laughter back by force. And he saw that Dr. and Mrs. Topman's faces were strangely blank and innocent, and that Cap'n Tom, Chuck's grandfather, quickly ran his hand over the lower part of his face as though to hide a smile.

Horatio's heart leaped. His mind boggled, so that for an instant he could not think at all. He could

57

not get his breath. What were the meaning of those smiles and nudges and innocent looks? Horatio gazed out across his audience and swallowed.

"But even if such a tiny planet existed," he said in a low, rather peculiar voice (and he forced a twinkle into his eye, for he must not give the game away as to what he had seen and what he suspected), "I do not believe that we could ever reach it. I defy anyone here to put up one good argument for the possibility of flying through space!"

Now a young physics professor started the ball rolling, and then Dr. Topman put in a word, and the arguments *for* space travel were followed by yells of delight from the children, and those against, by howls of dismay. And the discussion grew so hot (but everyone knew it was in fun) that they all had a marvelous time.

Then there were refreshments and everyone crowded around Horatio and eagerly went on with the argument while balancing cups of coffee, glasses of milk, and huge slices of Mrs. Topman's luscious fudge cake.

"If every meeting is going to be like this," exclaimed Dr. Topman, "the Society of Young Astronomers and Students of Space Travel is off to a *flying start!*"

"As Mr. Theodosius would say," whispered Chuck in David's ear, not wanting to get into a discussion with the others about the little man, "this Society sure takes the cake."

And indeed it did. In fact two cakes. And in another ten minutes, not a crumb was left of either of them.

CHAPTER 7

In the Dead of Night

ABOUT 10:30 that evening the boys conducted the beaming and self-satisfied Horatio back to 5 Thallo Street. He was extremely pleased with the results of his lecture.

"What a shame our friend Mr. Theodosius couldn't have been with us," cried Horatio gaily. "But then of course he is so deep in his work. What exactly," he went on innocently, "*is* his work? Or may I ask?"

"Oh, he's just going over some of Mr. Bass's experiments," answered David vaguely. "Everything Mr. Bass did was awfully complicated, so it's taking Mr. Theo a long time. But he'll get through them, all right, and he'll understand them too."

"You bet he will," said Chuck. "When Mr. Theo sets his mind to a thing, it is *done*."

"I see," said Horatio.

The boys left him in Mr. Bass's living room, where on the couch the blankets were turned back showing clean sheets and a pillow in a nice clean pillow case. All was ready for him to go to bed, but he did not go to bed. Nor did he even settle down to read after the boys had clattered off downstairs to see how Mr. Theodosius was coming along. For Horatio, sitting stiffly and nervously on the very edge of a chair, was remembering something.

He'd stolen off from the crowd around the refreshment table when he'd spied Chuck and David sniggering over in a corner, and then, right after that, he'd seen them disappear. He'd strolled over casually to get a handkerchief out of his overcoat pocket in the cloakroom, when from inside, where Mrs. Topman was unpacking another cake, he'd heard the most puzzling conversation.

"But *I* thought Professor Peabody was going to stay with *us*," she was saying.

"Yes — but, Mom, it'll be a lot safer with him over at Thallo Street. He won't bother anybody over there."

"Ten-fifteen! Good heavens, you boys ought to have been in bed long ago, considering what's ahead of you."

"But this is a special occasion," exclaimed David,

61

obviously trying to keep his voice down even though he seemed bursting with excitement. "Besides," and here his voice became a loud, raspy stage whisper, "we'll *sleep* all the way there and all the way back just the way we did last time. Remember?"

"And how about John and the children?" murmured his mother. "Is the coop ready for them?"

"Cap'n Tom finished it this afternoon," whispered Chuck. "There'll be that, and then the sacks of feed. They're awful heavy and awkward. Gee, I ought to know, after last time!"

And that was all! What could that conversation have meant? And who in the name of goodness were John and the children? And slept all the way to *where* and back? But now, in a flash, Chuck's question concerning planetoids combined unbelievably with this last baffling question of his own. Oh, but no! No! Horrified, Horatio's mind went snuffling and sidling up to the possibility of a voyage into space, then hastened, aghast, away again. No! The whole thing was simply laughable, beneath even a moment's thought. Two boys and a juggins of a leathery little old man like that Theodosius creature with his contrivances and contraptions down in the cellar . . .

Contrivances and contraptions! Horatio's mind

leaped up like a scared cat and came down again, quivering. He stared, unseeing, ahead of him. Some mischief was afoot, that he knew, for had not Dr. and Mrs. Topman looked innocent as babes? Far, far too innocent! Had not Cap'n Tom hid a smile? And hadn't the boys been sparkling with whatever secret it was they had? Could this whole thing, then, be tied up somehow with Mr. Bass's astound· ing discovery? And was *this* what Mr. Theo was working on?

Horatio, sitting shivering on the edge of his chair, realized that he would never know a moment's peace until he had found out the answer.

Quickly, quietly, he got up and arranged some clothes from his suitcase into a lump under the covers on the couch (he had seen two movies in his life, in one of which the hero had done this, and Horatio had always looked forward to being able to do it himself). Then he turned out the light, surveyed the lump that in the darkness looked exactly as if someone were lying there, then on tiptoe he slipped out of the house and around to the cellar door. Here he hunched down behind a bush and listened. The boys and Mr. Theo were talking, but all he could hear was:

"Well, then, a quarter of twelve, Mr. Theo.

Keep an eye on the clock — you've only got an hour. Anything we can do?"

"Not a thing, boys. You get all the necessities packed and ready at your end and then go down to the —"

"O.K.," interrupted Chuck eagerly, "we'll be there. Don't worry about us!"

Then out they came. But now David seemed t remember something of exceeding importance, for he turned suddenly and darted back into the cellar.

"Mr. Theo — Mr. Theo, did you remember the atomic tritetramethylbenzacarbonethylene in the fuel?"

"Yes, David, you may be sure I did!"

"Just *four drops*, Mr. Theo, for every pair of tanks?"

"Just four drops, David. *Plop! Plop! Plop! Plop!* No more, no less."

"Thank goodness! 'By, Mr. Theo. We'll see you."

The boys closed the cellar door behind them and hurried off down Thallo Street speaking in whispers. Horatio shuddered in the cold, damp night air. Atomic tritetramethyl — W H A T? Four drops in the fuel, in every pair of tanks! And *atomic*, the boy said! Great horrors!

Pondering the awful mystery of that explosive

word and its possible connection with whatever was afoot, Horatio settled himself grimly to wait until Mr. Theo should start off to wherever this meeting place was to be. An hour! And yet nothing on earth could have budged him.

Mr. Theo, however, emerged in a surprisingly short time with a big paintbrush, a bucket — full of something, for he carried it as if it were heavy — and an object that vaguely resembled a lantern. Away he went and, behind him at some distance, slipping like a thief from tree to tree, followed Horatio, darting, crouching, all the way down to the beach and Cap'n Tom's cave.

Once in the cave, Mr. Theo set down the bucket and brush. Then he lit the lantern that, by its unearthly soft yet penetrating radiance — the same weird radiance that flooded from those bubbles of light in Mr. Bass's cellar — revealed everything inside. And had not Mr. Theo been so intent upon prying the lid from his bucket of sealing mixture (fluid resinoid silicon, with other ingredients for treating the walls of the space ship), he would have heard an incredulous gasp. It was from someone who, in the darkness outside, was peering round the mouth of the cave and taking one bulging-eyed stare at something his reason had not allowed him to expect, but which now confirmed all his suspicions.

Horatio clapped his hands to his eyes, took another look, pinched himself, then shook his head. No, he was not dreaming — there it was, right before him: a space ship! There could not possibly be a mistake; he knew without a moment's doubt what it was: that smooth, wingless shape!

PART TWO

The Stowaway

CHAPTER 8

Farewell to Earth

At about twenty minutes of midnight, a procession was to be seen winding its way down the path from the Topman house to Cap'n Tom's beach. First came Chuck with John, the rooster, then David dragging a bag of chicken feed, then Mrs. Topman with a shopping bag of food and an auto robe. Behind her came Dr. Topman with the chicken coop in which, cackling and complaining, were already stowed the four pullets and one young cockerel who were the children of John and Mrs. Pennyfeather. Last of all came Cap'n Tom with two more sacks of feed on a light wheelbarrow.

They were speaking excitedly, but in low tones. Mrs. Topman was giving that lengthy advice to Chuck and David which mothers have always given to travelers, no matter how young or old, no matter where they may be traveling: down the street,

69

into the mountains, or across the world. It was all about keeping warm, keeping their feet dry, not eating too much (yet she had baked another cake and packed enough sandwiches for ten boys), not getting wet, not getting into drafts, not getting too tired, and being careful about cliffs and the strange country and strange insects and strange monsters. Meanwhile Chuck struggled with John, who was very wrought-up and not a bit sensible or peaceful the way Mrs. Pennyfeather had been when *she* was about to be snatched from the bosom of Mother Earth.

"Golly, Chuck," said David, "do you suppose Mrs. Pennyfeather'll remember us after all this time?"

"'Course she will," Chuck grunted, getting a firmer hold on John's wiry legs. "Why not? We've only been away a couple of months — not even that."

"Well, I know, but time goes so *fast* on Basidium. You know, what's a day there is a week here. Or, golly, is that right?" Now he began muttering to himself. "What's a day for them is a week for us because they *live* faster. Our week is squeezed into one Basidium day. Still — oh, heck, now I don't know *what* I think. Except I think I'm wrong!"

"You sure are!" shouted Chuck, then hastily smacked his hand over his mouth and thereby almost lost John. "You sure are," he whispered loudly at David, who was struggling over a rough place in the path with his bag of grain. "If Basidium turns faster, then they have *lots* of days while we only have one day. Any stupe would know that. Anyway, Mrs. Pennyfeather's no spore hen — she's an earth bird. So I bet she'll remember us."

On they went down the path, the grownups coming behind murmuring among themselves or just picking their way quietly around the turns and over the rocks. The little bent cypresses by the wayside rustled and hushed in the night breeze. Waves crashed below them along the shore with such force that the whole beach reverberated. The moon shone as radiantly as it had on that first memorable night of the take-off to Basidium; and now, as they rounded the last turn — there, far off down the beach, they saw something gleam, something flash. It was the space ship, and Mr. Theo was wheeling it out of the cave on its frame down to the big rock that stood, season after season, sometimes half buried in sand, sometimes black and naked and mountainous, on Cap'n Tom's beach. But by the time they had all got to Mr. Theo, huffing and puffing under their various burdens, the little man had got the space ship only halfway across the sand toward the rock.

"Tough going!" he gasped. "The ship's heavier than I thought. Oh, my — I'm *certainly* not the man I was, what with all this sitting around thinking and tinkering and not getting any exercise. *Tchk! Tchk!*" And he drew out an enormous handkerchief and mopped his brow.

Now Dr. Topman put down his chicken coop, and in no time at all he and little Mr. Theo had the ship down at the rock, which would serve as a sort of stepladder for the travelers when the ship was up-ended.

"How beautiful it is!" sighed Mrs. Topman, running her hand over the gleaming surface. "How very, very beautiful. And to think you two boys made it all by yourselves. I simply can't get it through my head."

Bursting with pride, and feeling secretly even a bit in awe of this incredible, silvery creature they had brought into being, Chuck and David, after a second's silence, began hopping with impatience.

"How about the fuel tanks, Mr. Theo?"

"And the sealer — is the sealer on — inside and out, Mr. Theo?"

72

"And the oxygen urn — how about the oxygen urn? And does it go phee-eep, phee-eep, Mr. Theo? It's just *got* to go phee-eep, phee-eep, or the trip won't seem a bit like last time."

"And the instrument that cuts off the rocket motor and turns us around in space so we'll land tail-first, Mr. Theo — you know, the reversatron — is that finished?"

"Everything is finished," smiled Mr. Theo. "Everything is just as it was before; you'll see. And now, gentlemen, as to our supplies. I think —"

"Oh boy!" yelled David, unable to restrain himself any longer and dashing over to the space ship and snatching open the door. "Come on! Let's get 'em in!"

"It's —" And Chuck whipped back his sleeve and took a quick look at his watch. "It's *eleven minutes of twelve* — and we've *got* to start at midnight precisely, or we won't make it."

"Avast there!" rumbled Cap'n Tom, coming over and laying a large, calming hand on Chuck's shoulder. "We must upend her first and *then* put in the supplies. Otherwise we shall have a mess in the hold."

"But, Grandpop," protested Chuck, "we have to strap everything down *anyway*, so's, when we get out beyond gravity, all the sacks of feed and the chicken coop and John won't float around inside the ship and bang us on the heads."

"B' the great white whale — I'd forgot that. I'm so used to seagoing ships!" And Cap'n Tom, somewhat embarrassed, rubbed his hand back and forth across his chin.

"Yes," said Mr. Theo, "we'll stow everything away now, lash it all down, and *then* we'll upend her."

Almost in silence, except for the occasional cackle or squawk of a puzzled and frightened fowl and the grunts of Cap'n Tom and Dr. Topman as they hoisted the bags of grain, the necessities of the journey were stored away in the ship and strapped into place. When the sacks were in, the chicken coop was wedged firmly between them, the big shopping bag of food was placed handily to the travelers' seats with the auto robe pushed underneath. Then John was tied by his legs to the top of the coop, being too large and unruly to put inside, and now he stood there jerking about and angrily complaining to anyone who would listen, his comb bobbing and quivering with rage.

Last of all, little Mr. Theo came back from the

74

cave dragging a rather large box by a rope handle; when Mr. Topman heaved it up into the ship, it rattled.

"What's in it?" shouted David. "What's *in* that box, Mr. Theo?"

"Ah," said Mr. Theo, and he winked at the boys, "that's *my* secret." Then he popped into the space ship and could be heard securing the box firmly near the oxygen urn.

Now at last Chuck, David, Mr. Theo and Dr. Topman and Cap'n Tom all stationed themselves near the nose of the ship and then began shoving up strongly from underneath. As they pushed, they moved gradually back toward the rear.

"Steady, boys, steady!" sang out Cap'n Tom.

"Steady, ste-ea-dy!"

"Careful!" cried Mrs. Topman.

Up, up went the ship, and for just a moment after she had been pushed upright onto her tail, the little group stood and gazed at that long, slim nose pointing straight up into the velvety sky all sparkling with stars.

Then David gave his mother a quick hug and the two boys scrambled up the rock, got in at the door of the ship and strapped themselves to their seats, which were to the right of Mr. Theo's. Then Mr.

Theo, having been handed his tall hat, set it upon his head at a particularly jaunty angle, drew from his pocket his gloves (carefully washed and mended by Mrs. Topman), flung his cloak about his shoulders, darted up the rock, sprang in and slipped into his place. Now there were hurried, muffled good-bys, a last anxious reminder from Mrs. Topman, the door was finally closed and bolted tight, and then — all was ready.

The three remaining figures on the beach hurried off to a distance as the second of midnight, precisely, drew near. Chuck and David crouched down, gritted their teeth, and screwed up their faces, and then Mr. Theo, having eagerly sung out the final passing seconds, was about to press the button, when —

"Great, jumping Jehoshaphat — the lantern!" he shouted. "I *must* have it — Tyco's lantern!"

"No time, Mr. Theo — no time!" yelled Chuck desperately, beating Mr. Theo on the arm. "Pull her back — pull the stick — *we've got to go!*"

"*Lantern!*" insisted Mr. Theo, and shoving Chuck and David aside, he reached over and got the door open again. "*Lantern!*" he bellowed in such tones as they'd never dreamed such a tiny man could use.

In a breath Dr. Topman had run over, snatched up the lantern, and scrambled up the rock. Then once more the door was bolted tight, and the moment Dr. Topman had got far enough away, Mr. Theo pressed the button, pulled back the stick — and all was blinding confusion and a single hideous, shattering roar.

As the space ship streaked upward, faster and faster, Dr. and Mrs. Topman and Cap'n Tom stood frozen to stillness, staring up into the skies where that streak of flame dwindled, dwindled — and finally vanished altogether.

The boys and Mr. Theo were gone from the earth.

"Oh, my," murmured Mrs. Topman, her hand up to her mouth, "oh, my — I *do* hope they will be careful!"

"Never," got out Cap'n Tom dazedly, "did an old sea dog like me ever expect to be present at the launching of such a ship."

Only Dr. Topman was silent, and then finally was heard to mutter to himself, "Fifty thousand miles!" Mrs. Topman looked at him.

"Fifty thousand miles, fiddlesticks," she said briskly. "*One hundred thousand miles*, what with the return journey."

Now the three of them turned and walked slowly back across the deserted beach. The waves still crashed and resounded along the shore, the moon still shone in a broad path across the ocean. And on the spot by the big rock where the space ship had stood was a great pit of blackened sand, scattered with lumps of silica which had melted and hardened into glass as though some giant lightning bolt had struck there.

Ah, but where was the figure that had so recently crouched in the bushes at the mouth of the cave, shivering with cold but as well with some awful dread? The figure was gone. And oddly enough it had not been there since just before Mr. Theo had wheeled the space ship out across the sand.

CHAPTER 9

Chuck and David's
First Fight

Now the space ship had settled to its steady, smooth, absolutely noiseless flight, the oxygen urn to its steady phee-eep, phee-eep, and John and the chickens to only an occasional cluck or cry. John, temporarily, seemed quite broken in spirit by what he had recently been through. And as for Mr. Theo, he was gazing in stunned silence all about him at the sight that met his eyes out of the big window of the space ship.

"No," the boys heard him say to himself as he caught his breath, "even on the highest peaks of the Himalayas, I have never beheld a sight to equal this."

The constellations visible at this hour of night in the June sky were Virgo, Libra, the Corona Borealis, Boötes, and Leo. But so crowded and lost were they in a sea of suns that only a practiced eye could have pointed out their ancient, gigantic shapes.

"Look!" cried Mr. Theo. "There ahead and a little to the left is Arcturus, the most brilliant, blazing star of all."

"How far away is Arcturus, Mr. Theo?"

"About forty light-years, Chuck — 240 trillion miles — "

"Arcturus must be awful huge to shine so bright in the midst of all those stars."

"It's more than a thousand times larger than our sun. And even at the speed it's going — about ninety miles an hour — it would take a thousand years for us to see that it has moved at all. Now, look — out there in the constellation Virgo is another brilliant star, Spica. And up there, to the left of Arcturus and above it, is the Northern Crown, or the Corona Borealis, and 'way round on our other side, down there to the right, is Regulus in the constellation Leo."

The boys looked and looked, and all that was spread before them seemed even more beautiful, more wondrous, than it had the other time. David could not understand this, having promised himself that nothing could ever be as good as that first flight to Basidium, simply because it *had* been the first. But now, even though he had looked forward to this moment with such intensity for so many weeks, it *was* as good — it was even better. And he had to tell himself again and again, "I'm here — I'm really here at last, in our space ship, speeding at the rate of 25,000 miles an hour out beyond the earth into space."

But Chuck was beginning to feel dizzy as he stared at those far-distant suns. Suddenly he had to bring himself back to ordinary things again by remarking happily how nice and comforting it was to hear the pheeping of the oxygen urn because it sounded exactly the way it had the first time.

"I must tell you something funny about that," said Mr. Theo. "When I had finished the urn, I was terribly disappointed to find, when I turned it on, that it made no noise whatever. Knowing how you boys would have felt about that, I had to take the spigot off and ever so slightly squeeze one of the little pipes with my pliers. And lo and behold, when I turned the spigot on again — it pheeped!"

"Oh, what a re —" began David, when all at once Mr. Theo, with a startled look on his face, held up his hand for silence.

The boys listened, and to their incredulous and

shocked amazement, another sound intruded itself, beside the pheeping of the urn and the low murmuring of the chickens, which was not right or familiar at all. It was a scuffling sound, hard and awkward, and then — and then — could it be? — what sounded like actual words, words such as "Stifling to death" and "Twisted into a knot" and *"Get me out of here!"*

Instantly Mr. Theo turned his flashlight to the very rear of the space ship, and there in its gleam was revealed, sticking out from behind the oxygen urn, the white, desperate, terrified face of Horatio Q. Peabody.

There was a moment of horrified silence. Their privacy had been invaded — *and* by trickery, by means most sly and contemptible! The thought even flashed into David's head that now, perhaps, the flight to Basidium might never be completed, or that it would end in disaster because an Outsider had been brought along. Mr. Bass had said, the first time, "Only children can do this thing!" And of course Mr. Theo was one of the Basses, a Basidiumite himself, so *he* was all right. But this Peabody person, this unbeliever, this *stranger* . . . It was unthinkable.

Now there was an upraising of furious, accusing

voices, the boys calling Horatio all sorts of villain, and Horatio simply staring at them in angry silence, while Mr. Theo called for a little peace and quiet. From under the seat he pulled a coil of rope, which he threw to Horatio so that Horatio could lash himself down next to the chicken coop, there being no pull of gravity to keep him down once he let go of it. But Horatio missed, and the rope, carried by the force of Mr. Theo's throw to the end of the ship, bounced against the oxygen urn and then floated around in the most ridiculous fashion.

"Look at that!" muttered Chuck in bitter disgust. "He can't even catch anything."

Finally, however, Horatio managed to get hold of an end of it and tied himself down into as comfortable a position as possible in those crowded quarters. But John was practically on top of him and studied him first with one cold, round, orange eye and then the other, while the hens and the cockerel, inquisitive young things, kept poking their beaks cozily over his shoulder and under his ear.

At last Horatio spoke.

"When the truth began to dawn on me," he began in a low voice, "that Tyco Bass's discovery had something to do with a satellite of earth's, that you believed in this satellite, and that you were actually planning to go there, then I knew that I, too, must go in order to find out the truth or nonsense of this business for myself. I —"

"*Nonsense!*" exploded Chuck, almost beside himself. "Why, we've not only *seen* this satellite, we've—" But Mr. Theo quickly laid a restraining hand against Chuck's mouth and David gave a cry to drown his words.

"I still do not believe in your satellite," went on Horatio coolly. "I believe that we are doomed. But I had to go. I knew that it would be hopeless to *ask* to go, and so, for the sake of Science —" And now Horatio leaned forward and spoke in penetrating tones: "For the sake of Science, I say, I determined to subject myself to any danger, to the anger I would of course arouse, so that I might see for myself, and hand on to the public at large, whatever this discovery of Tyco Bass's turned out to be."

"But *how* . . . ?"

"*When* did you . . . ?"

"I waited outside the mouth of the cave while you, Mr. Theodosius Bass, stirred and stirred that — that *concoction* of yours which you saw fit to slap all over the inside and outside of the ship. What good you think it will do, I can't imagine. At any rate, I held my breath for fear you would paint the outside first. But, no — in you went, and when you emerged and went to the other side where you were hidden from me — and I from you — in a trice I had crept within and hidden myself behind the oxygen urn. What I went through after that, the terror I endured, I shall never be able to describe to anyone —"

"I declare!" exclaimed Mr. Theo. "*That's* why the space ship was so confoundedly heavy to push across the sand!"

"But you had no *right* —" shouted David and Chuck, and then were silenced by Horatio's upraised hand and his sudden, harsh, loud, relentless voice.

"Do not speak of *rights*," he cried. "None of us have any *rights* when it comes to Science. We serve her. Whatever Mr. Bass's secret is, it belongs to the world — it is the world's possession. And as soon as I have seen this satellite, explored it, taken copious notes, digested them and got them into order, I intend to write a long, detailed, absolutely *sound* scientific paper about it. *That is my duty!*"

"*Your duty!*" cried Chuck in a fury. "You won't be able to prove a thing, not without Mr. Bass's filter —"

"Oh, shut up, Chuck! *Shut up!*" burst out David

85

in angry despair. But already he saw how all this would turn out. Someone who had absolutely no understanding would see Basidium and the Mushroom People with his own eyes — and would tell the whole thing. Then there would be the awful publicity, the papers would be full of it, the peace and quiet of Pacific Grove would be shattered, Mr. Bass's little house would be trampled and overrun with newspapermen, and he and Chuck would be questioned for hours for news of this unbelievable discovery. The necklace of Ta and the marvelous Stroboscopic Polarizing Filter would be taken from them and put on display. Nothing would be secret any more. Even he and Chuck, probably, would be forced to go on display.

"Surely," Horatio was saying with a scornful laugh, "surely you don't expect me to take this story about a filter seriously. A planet is either present in the heavens, or it is not present, filter or no filter — and that's all there is to it."

"Well, that's just how stupid *you* are," yelled Chuck, deaf now to any entreaty from David. "Why do you suppose no astronomer's ever discovered Basidium before, a little old planetoid only 50,000 miles out from earth where nobody could miss it? Because he *couldn't* discover it, that's why! Not

without Mr. Bass's Stroboscopic Polarizing Filter —
so there! And we've got it. And nobody else'll *ever*
get it!"

"Indeed," returned Horatio levelly. "Then it is
your duty, in the interests of astronomy, to give it
up, to allow all astronomers to profit by Mr. Bass's
good luck. Not in the interests of low commerce —
no! — but in the interests of posterity. If you hold
back the filter, if you hold back proof of the existence of this Basidium, as you call it, then you hold
up the progress of Science. Do you *dare* to do that?
No one — not even Einstein, nor any great man —
would ever have had the courage to do it."

Poor Chuck clapped his fists over his ears, looking
miserably unhappy, terrified of what Horatio might
make him believe. But David by this time was boil-
ing mad.

"Well, you listen to me, Professor Peabody. I
don't believe you're so determined to get to Basidium just for the sake of Science. You just want in
on the secret. You just want to blow up your own
reputation. And you'll *never* get the filter. Maybe,
sometime, astronomers will have it — but not yet.
Mr. Bass said that. He said *the right time would
come.*"

"Ta was good to us," broke in Chuck. "He's the

87

king of the Mushroom People, and he gave us his own necklace because we saved them. He'd hate it if we took outsiders there. The Basidiumites'd die of fright. I don't know *what* he'll say when he sees you! We've already thought: What if huge space ships went there someday and took tourists back and forth?"

"Tourists!" spat out Horatio in disgust. "I despise tourists." And then his eyes gleamed. "On the other hand, what if I could lead an expedition — a scientific expedition —"

But now David, because the whole thing was becoming more and more frightful as Horatio rattled on with his plans, suddenly turned to Chuck because he had to vent his rage somewhere.

"It's all your fault, Chuck Masterson," he shouted, seeing Chuck as detestable for the first time in his life. "You let it all out because of the silly way you acted at the lecture. You acted like a sap and an idiot. Professor Peabody said there was no life on other planets, especially not on planetoids, and that we'd be smashed to jelly traveling through space to get there, and every time he said something, you giggled and poked me and looked smart — a regular old saphead — gave it all away! I *saw* you!"

Chuck turned and stared at David, and then his brows came together and his face darkened.

"Listen! I wasn't the only one. So did you give things away. Don't talk to me about being a sap when you were the first —"

"I was not —"

Out flew David's fist, and then Chuck's, and before the boys knew it they were punching with their knuckles, hate springing hot between them, and all awkward and ridiculous because they were strapped to their seats and had to twist sideways.

Oddly enough, Mr. Theo, who had simply listened quietly and thoughtfully to all this, made no move to stop them.

But suddenly, as they grabbed one another, the necklace of Ta flew from David's pocket and floated away, and the boys turned and saw Horatio snatch at it and then snap on his flashlight. Strapped down as they were, they could not reach far enough to keep the necklace from him.

"Give it back!"

"It's ours — give it back!"

But Horatio sat without moving, his mouth slightly open, as he gazed wordlessly at the shimmering stones which he held up in his left hand.

CHAPTER 10

Worse Than Nothingness

UNAWARE, apparently, of the boys' cries of frustration, Horatio continued to hold up the necklace of Ta, as though he could not believe what he saw, and all the while Mr. Theo's shrewd eyes were upon him.

"*Why* did you bring it, Dave?" wailed Chuck.

"I don't know — I guess I was afraid somebody just might bust into Mr. Bass's house and break open the safe while we were gone. They wouldn't know *what* the filter was — just a lump of glass maybe — and his notebooks look as if they're filled with scribbles. But the necklace —"

"The jewels of Basidium!" Horatio got out at last. "It's fantastic, that's what it is." Then he looked up as though something had just dawned on him, and he muttered words to himself, words that sounded to David like ". . . mining operations, of course! To supply the funds for research . . ."

Mining operations on Basidium!

"Oh, no, you won't." And David made another futile lunge. "Nobody's doing any mining on our planet."

Mr. Theo smiled.

"Perhaps you ought to return it to the boys now, Professor Peabody. I don't imagine you would want to keep what isn't yours."

Horatio held out the necklace with dignity.

"Naturally, I have no intention of keeping it. What would be the purpose? And may I say that, to me, it was an extremely embarrassing sight to behold two old friends fighting as you boys did just now? What could I have said to cause such savage emotions? Simply that I intend exploring Basidium thoroughly in order to preserve for the future this historic expedition. Ye-e-es. . . ." And here Horatio's face changed and became filled with wonder and delight.

"Why, just think, it *could* be one of the two *great* scientific papers of the twentieth century: Einstein's 'Explanation of the Theory of Relativity,' and Horatio Peabody's 'Exploration of a Hitherto Unknown Second Satellite'!"

"Indeed," assented Mr. Theo gravely, "and no doubt you, its author, would become One with the

Ages — a most humbling thought, is it not, Professor Peabody?"

Horatio, bright-eyed, nodded with great solemnity. He must be absolutely blind, thought David. He doesn't even realize that Mr. Theo's just teasing him. Why, you could feed him whole bucketfuls of flattery and he'd swallow it all.

"Now, boys," continued Mr. Theo, "as we have to finish our journey in such close quarters, we'll have to get along together. Do you think you could possibly be friends again?"

"I'm sorry, Chuck."

"Me, too, Dave." Whereupon they shook hands in a certain private way of their own as they always did on state occasions. "I even saw Grandpop smile at the lecture, and your mother and dad looked at each other, and Professor Peabody must have been watching them. I don't think it was *anybody's* fault — not any one person's."

"We've got to cooperate!" cried Horatio, leaning forward eagerly. "Picture to yourself if *you* were an astronomer on the verge of a momentous revelation. Be fair! Be honest! Can you blame me for what I have done?"

But while Chuck and David were frowning in an enormous effort to be fair and honest, Mr. Theo all at once gave a laugh that was like a soft high rush of wind in the trees.

"Professor Peabody, you have no idea of the momentous revelations Tyco Bass had up his sleeve — or rather between the pages of his notebook. For instance, from what I gathered in his notes, he had come upon something which I've already mentioned, but to which you refused to pay any attention except to laugh at me. You may remember that I said I felt as if I were plunging through a hole in space when I studied his writings and realized the range of his busy mind. I didn't say that idly, for Tyco *had* actually convinced himself of that possibility: a *hole in space!*"

So unexpected was the end of Mr. Theo's sentence, that there was a stunned gasp from his three listeners. Chuck and David could not reply, but at last Horatio gathered himself and spoke.

"*Uf!*" he snorted, a kind of scornful grunt. "Really, Mr. Theodosius, this is nothing but childish prattle. Space *is* a hole. How can there be a hole inside a hole?"

Mr. Theo spread his hands.

"I really don't know," he replied. "I am not the man my cousin is. But apparently long ago he had begun to be suspicious that such a thing exists, and then his filter confirmed these suspicions. I presume that by now he has full knowledge of this phenomena. Yes, I am certain that if we could only speak to Tyco, he would be able to tell us all about it."

A *hole in space*, David repeated to himself. Why did those words strike terror to the very marrow of his soul? At this moment he was in a space ship, hurtling through nothingness. Surely this hole could be no worse than nothingness. Then why this cold horror? He did not know. He tried hard to picture what a hole in space would be like, but he really could not.

"Where is this thing, then?" Horatio asked with amused indifference, meanwhile drawing a pen out of his breast pocket and fumbling about in the other pockets of his coat for something else. "Where in the universe does this monstrosity of Tyco Bass's lie, or did he say?"

"Oh, yes," replied Mr. Theo lightly. "Yes, he did. And you might be interested to know, Professor Peabody, that it isn't far off the vector we're traveling along. You could put that down in your notes and then later work it into that scientific paper of yours — the great scientific paper of the twentieth century."

"But, Mr. Theo," burst out Chuck, "is there —

is there any chance we'll plunge into it?"

"Oh, no, no, my boy," replied Mr. Theo comfortably. "But the movement of this hole is an orbit around the earth, just as the movement of Basidium is. And this hole moves *between* the earth and Basidium. Therefore it determined Tyco's planning of your journey and the timing of it."

"You mean, then," said David slowly, "that no matter how anybody figured and figured and figured, the only directions to follow to get to Basidium and back to Pacific Grove again, are the ones Mr. Bass worked out — because of the orbit of this hole getting in the way, and the different speeds of the earth, and the hole, and Basidium."

"That's it. I did a vast deal of figuring, but I couldn't get any different answer to Tyco's without getting mixed up in the orbit of that hole, which is tarnation tricky."

There was a little silence, and then the boys heard, in addition to the pheeping of the oxygen urn and the low murmurings of the hens, what sounded like a small scratching. They turned and there they saw that Horatio Q. Peabody, by the gleam of his flashlight which he had rigged up on the chicken coop, was busy taking notes for all he was worth in a very impressive-looking notebook.

CHAPTER 11

The Disappearance
of Mebe and Oru

I⟙ did not seem possible they could have been asleep — one moment they were listening to the ominous scratching of Horatio's pen, and the next they were being awakened by Mr. Theo, shaking them. The first thing David thought was, "We're still here! We didn't fall into the hole after all!" Then he saw that the light was a pale, delicate blue-green and when he spoke it was in the language of Basidium which, strangely enough, seemed familiar and well-known to him, though it had been some time since he had spoken it last and then only for two hours.

"We've got it back again, Dave — we've got it! Remember how many times we tried to remember the word for 'star' in Basidiumite, or 'earth' or 'water' or 'fire'? And we couldn't get any of it back, not a whisper."

"I feel as though I'd spoken it always — now that I'm speaking it again," David said.

"And I!" cried Mr. Theo. There was the oddest look on Mr. Theo's face — a mingling of intense surprise and joy and unbelief. "It seems to me," he said, "that I have spoken this language in my dreams, with this voice. It's a strange language, yet perfectly natural to me. It's my own, of course, and yet it can't be possible I've ever really spoken it. Everything is familiar somehow — this light, for instance, this beautiful blue-green light!"

Now the boys looked round to see what Horatio might be up to, and he was still fast asleep with his pen and notebook held loosely in his fingers. He was no longer alert and determined and busy, and David was just wondering if it would be right to snatch the notebook from him — when Horatio suddenly jerked erect. He blinked, stared at the green light, then muttered something — frowned in amazement — and muttered something else, a little more loudly. Plainly he could not believe what he heard.

"My throat!" he croaked, clutching his throat with both hands. And the result of that cry was somehow enormously funny to the boys, because Horatio's voice had become soft and high as any

Mushroom Person's so that the croak he uttered was a soft, high, far-off croak. But his expression now turned from amazement to terror. "What has happened? Where are we?" And, tied as he was, he tried to leap up, struggling vainly.

"Take it easy, Professor Peabody," said Chuck. "We're just about to land on Basidium, that's all. And your voice has changed to a Mushroom voice and you're speaking Basidiumite. There's nothing to worry about."

Horatio stared at Chuck.

"Basidiumite!" he gasped. "But what if I don't *wish* to speak Basidiumite? What if I wish to speak — to speak —" But of course Horatio could not say "English" because there is no word in Basidiumite for "English." "I can't seem to remember. . . . What has happened to me?" Poor Horatio looked as if he were going out of his mind.

"Nothing has happened to you, Professor. Only you can't speak the other language. You've forgotten it, just for now. Every word you say'll come out Basidiumite. And when you get back to earth, you'll have forgotten the language of Basidium — and you'll feel very sad, the way we did."

Horatio held up his hand and looked at it.

"Hand," they heard him mutter anxiously. But

no, what he said could not, by any stretch of the imagination, be called English. "Foot. Leg," he cried in this strange tongue. "Man. Writing instrument. *I am a man!*" Then, as though he simply didn't know what to make of it all, he turned and stared at John. "*Winged creature!*" exclaimed Horatio, and then a look of surprise came over his face, for he had no doubt wanted to say "rooster," for which the Mushroom People have no word.

For a moment, Horatio looked off at nothing, as though he were thinking very hard about all this. Then he took up his pen and began writing it down: the feelings of a man who has forgotten his own language completely and is speaking an unknown tongue without being able to help it.

Now they plunged, tail downward, through the winding green mists toward Basidium, and Chuck and David watched, too excited to speak. Then, as they neared the surface, more slowly because Mr. Theo had increased the rocket power to lessen the force of landing, the boys were amazed to see a tiny figure waiting as though to greet them. Now the figure raised its arm in a gesture of eager welcome.

"Dave, it's Ta! Mr. Theo, look, look — that's Ta, the king of the Mushroom People. He's come to meet us. But — *how did he know?*"

The ship came down with a soft jolt and thud, and Ta came majestically forward, his arms out and his pale green face alight with joy. Then the door was unbolted and out leaped Chuck and David. Ta grasped their hands, crying how good it was to see them again, and the boys in their turn found it very hard to remember that Ta was a king and that they must show him deference. Instead they jumped up and down all around him, pumping his hands in a most undignified fashion.

"We'd have been here ages before this," shouted Chuck, "if we could've just built a ship, but we had to wait —"

"You see, *our* ship, Great Ta, the one you saw before," explained David, his words tumbling over one another in his effort to get everything out at once, "got smashed up, and so we thought we'd never see you again. But then who should come along but Mr. Theo, Tyco Bass's cousin. See, there he is — up there," and David waved toward the door of their space ship where Mr. Theo was to be seen, leaning out and gazing at Basidium with a look of the most supreme happiness on his little Basidiumite face. And it was a face that, strangely enough, now that he was on the Mushroom Planet, seemed faintly greenish — greenish as is the flesh of all Mushroom People — and his thin, long-fingered hands as well. Or is it simply an effect of the green light? David wondered.

"But surely he is one of our kinsmen!" murmured Ta, in the utmost amazement. "Surely I know him —"

Now Ta strode over to the ship, kingly and upright, unmistakably a Personage even though he was, like Mr. Theo, scarcely taller than the two boys. And then Mr. Theo, having lowered the chicken coop to the ground by means of a rope, jumped out — light as a mushroom spore — and the two little men clasped each other's hands tightly, tightly, as though they were old friends, or as though they had been brothers.

"This is my homeland!" exclaimed Mr. Theo. "This is the place I've searched for all my life. Now I can be at rest. Here is where I stay."

"Welcome!" said Ta, overcome with emotion. "I welcome you!"

But at Mr. Theo's words, the boys looked at him, appalled.

"You mean you're not going *back* with us, Mr. Theo — and we've only just found you?"

Mr. Theo nodded his head regretfully, and yet

he was smiling and looked more peaceful than they had ever seen him.

Now, red and gasping, there appeared in the doorway of the space ship the angry face of Horatio Q. Peabody, quite plainly furious at having been left to struggle out of his awkward tied-up position by himself. He jumped down — and stared thunderstricken all around, and at sight of him Ta's face darkened for the first time.

"Who is this?" demanded Ta sternly.

"He is a stowaway, Great Ta," explained David. "That means we didn't intend to bring him, but he got into the ship when no one was looking and we didn't know he was there until after we'd started."

Horatio could scarcely contain himself. He stared at the great mushrooms towering above his head, big as trees some of them, pink and cream and gray with flutings on the underside of dark brown — giant replicas of the smaller mushrooms that grew everywhere. Strange primitive-looking plants were mingled with them, plants that had palmlike, feathery fronds, plants reminding David of the trees that had existed when dinosaurs inhabited the earth. Everywhere underfoot spread the green, damp moss that carpets Basidium over the entire extent of its lower altitudes. But what seemed to stagger Horatio, what he could not seem to get over, was the enormous shape of earth hanging, veiled in winding green mists, in the sky of Basidium. Softly, its reflected light, like that of some unthinkably huge moon, silvered the mists. The sun was not to be seen — only the overwhelming earth. And Horatio stood and stared at it with his mouth open.

Then at last he snatched out his notebook and scratched and scratched across its pages as though he were possessed. And suddenly Ta, who had been following all Horatio's peculiar actions with astonishment, put back his head and shouted with laughter.

"This person is funny. He amuses me. Let him stay. But bring him before me and tell me what he is called."

So Horatio was brought forward and introduced, but to David's horror he seemed determined to give no sign that Ta was a king.

"How do you do?" he said, sticking out his hand roughly, with no show of ceremony at all.

"These words — *how do you do?* — I do not know," returned Ta gravely. His face was unsmiling, but in his eyes there was the smallest twinkle. Then, with both hands held together, he touched Horatio's hand, and after that held up his right arm and said, "I greet you, visitor from the Great Protector which you call by the name of earth."

And somehow, in spite of Horatio's refusal to bow to Ta, to show him respect and deference, and in spite of the fact that he was so much the taller of the two, Ta was still the kingly one. He is still, thought David, the one who is the Personage, and Horatio Q. Peabody seems without manners compared to him.

Now, to David's further horror, Horatio suddenly bent forward and stared closely at Ta's face, and then at Ta's hands.

"*Green,* by all the great gods!" he burst out, in that grating voice of his. "Is every one of you *green?*" he demanded, and scribbled it down, muttering to himself. Then, while Ta watched him with a strange, faint smile on his lips, and while Mr. Theo looked on with the same amused expression, Horatio suddenly snatched up a fold of Ta's long garment — half transparent, soft, cream-colored, and of the texture of very thin rubber, or plastic.

"Like the stuff they make bags of to keep things fresh, in the — in the — in the *food box,*" murmured Horatio, scratching away furiously in his notebook.

"Now, tell me, sir — how do you make it — you know, how do you fix it up like this?"

But David could feel his temperature rising.

"You're not to speak to Ta that way," he interrupted angrily. "You may be a professor, but you're a guest here. Don't you stare like that, and snatch up people's clothes. It isn't polite."

Horatio ignored this, but Ta gave what sounded like a chuckle. Then he explained to Horatio very courteously how the flesh of the bilba trees (the tallest of the mushrooms) was shredded and beaten and soaked and dried and then rolled out flat until it looked as his garment did. Scratch, scratch, scratch, went Horatio's tireless pen. Then Ta said they must all go back to the village, for he had a surprise for them.

"A surprise!" exclaimed Chuck. "Oh, boy —"

"But how could you have a surprise for us, Great Ta, unless you knew we were coming?" asked David, and then remembered how Ta had been there, waiting for them to arrive. He felt queer suddenly, a little frightened. "*Did* you know we were coming?"

Ta put his hand on David's shoulder.

"Yes, David," he replied. "I knew. A friend of yours told me. But you shall find out all about that later."

"Thought transference," muttered Horatio, and wrote it down.

"C'mon, Dave — let's get John and the children. *Boy*, won't Mrs. Pennyfeather be glad to see her family! How is she, Great Ta — how's Mrs. Pennyfeather? Is she all right? Did she lay lots of Magic Stones? Do Mebe and Oru, your Wise Men, cook them all right now, and do your people like them — the Magic Stones, that is?"

But at Chuck's question, an expression of great sadness came over Ta's face.

"Yes," he said. "Mrs. Pennyfeather is fine and healthy. She lives in great state, as you shall see, and is almost worshiped by my people, having saved their lives. We have many of the sulfur plants, as our last crop was good, but we would have died had it not been for the gifts you made possible while we waited for new sulfur plants to grow. But it is not Mebe and Oru who cook the Magic Stones."

There was a small, tense silence, broken only by Horatio's muttering and the relentless sound of his pen.

"Sulfur plants," he was heard to say to himself. "Apparently of great importance. Necessity to health. Magic Stones — Basidiumite name — wor-

106

ship of a winged creature — inquire into this —"

But David and Chuck were staring at Ta, their faces grave, almost stern.

"What has become of Mebe and Oru, Great Ta?" asked David. "You promised us — that is, I remember you saying that you would allow Mebe and Oru to live, that you would not punish them for their carelessness in letting the sulfur plants die without discovering anything to take their place. You haven't — after all . . . ?" But David could not go on. Mebe and Oru — such funny little men! So helpless for Wise Men, so unwise, and yet so lovable. David waited in horror for Ta to speak. ("We're to have our heads cut off in the morning — *squirp!*" David remembered little Oru had cried.)

"Mebe and Oru have disappeared," replied Ta in a low voice. "But, come. Let us go back to the village at once, and I will tell you what happened as we go along." Now Mr. Theo and Ta drew together, Ta taking Mr. Theo's arm as though he had known him always. Horatio went on ahead, staring about and writing constantly, just as fast he could.

And as soon as Chuck and David had got a good hold on John, they stuffed him in the coop with his children and carried it along between them.

107

First of all, related Ta, it had preyed on the minds of Mebe and Oru that they had failed in their task of doing something about the loss of the sulfur plants. Then, after David and Chuck had gone from Basidium, leaving Mrs. Pennyfeather, Mebe had dropped one of her Magic Stones and broken it. Then Oru had boiled one of them for too short a time, so that when he opened it, the insides were still soft. Thus it had been wasted, for the Basidiumites simply could not eat soft eggs. Last of all, the two little men had sat up all night reading over their Rolls of Wisdom, had decided they'd accomplished nothing in their lives, and had gone off into the mountains the next day never to return.

"So the note said," finished Ta sadly, "that they left propped up on the seat of my throne for me to find when I got up in the morning. Now I have two new Wise Men: Keeg and Oique — very dignified, very sensible. They never say foolish things, they never drop the Magic Stones, nor overcook, nor undercook them. They are fine, upstanding Wise Men — but oh, how they bore me! They are so efficient in such an uninteresting way. They never make me laugh. I wish my little Wise Men would come back."

108

"And have you sent out a search party for them?" inquired Mr. Theo.

"Indeed I have — but with no results. And I was about to get up another with myself at the head when I was told of your coming. But I must not cloud your welcome with my troubles — forgive me."

David and Chuck looked at one another across the chicken coop out of which John had angrily and indignantly stuck his head.

"Great Ta! Will you let Chuck and me go on this search party with you? And Mr. Theo? Perhaps, just as we were able to save your people last time, we'll be able somehow to find Mebe and Oru."

"I *betcha* we could!" shouted Chuck excitedly. "I just *betcha*! And Mr. Theo's the greatest traveler the world has ever known. Why, he —"

But just then Ta held up his arm, and there, coming along the roadway toward them, they saw a whole crowd of Basidiumites, their green faces shining with happiness, and their voices raised in cries of welcome. In their hands they carried what looked like shining yellow flutes.

CHAPTER 12

Escape from
the Mushroom People

"WHY, they're made of gold!" cried Horatio, going up to the Basidiumites and devouring with his eager, excited gaze the beautiful instruments which the Mushroom People carried. And something in his voice, something greedy and wild, sent a start of troubled uneasiness over David.

The Mushroom People were frightened. At sight of the huge stranger, who must have seemed a giant to them, they crowded back in alarm. Mr. Theo, even with his dark, tall hat on, which he wore so jauntily, they did not seem to mind, as he looked so much like themselves.

Once more Ta held up his arm.

"Do not be afraid, my people," he cried. "Our saviors from the Great Protector have returned, and they have promised to help us search for our Wise

Men. This large person came with them." Here Ta paused for a second and settled a peculiar glance on Horatio Q. Peabody which it was impossible to read. "Our guests promise us that he is friendly and means no harm. We are to trust him. As for my companion here," and now Ta turned to Mr. Theo and drew him forward, whereupon Mr. Theo removed his top hat and smiled at the Basidiumites, "he is one of our long lost kinsmen. Welcome him warmly, for he is one of us. He has come home — he is here to stay!"

"*Yiy!*" shouted all the little Basidiumites. "*Yiy-aye-yiy!*" And putting their flutes to their lips, they turned back toward the village, playing all the way, while some of them hummed in a high, wavering key so that it was as if a hundred sea-winds were all sighing and crying together.

"Their flutes," demanded Horatio, oblivious of this lovely sound, "they *are* of gold, aren't they?"

"We have much of that shining substance in our high places," replied Ta indifferently, "and in various colors, as you perhaps noticed. The greenish flutes are high in tone, the yellowish are middle-toned, and the reddish ones are deep-toned. Do you make music on the Great Protector?"

111

But Horatio did not answer. He was staring straight ahead and seemed to be thinking deeply.

So they arrived in the little city, a place of many small igloo-shaped houses, of which Ta's palace was the largest. Now other Basidiumites came out to greet the boys. When they exclaimed in fright at the sight of Horatio, Ta once more told how the stranger meant no harm, and would leave when the boys went away again in the creature of silver.

Meanwhile Horatio was beside himself with the effort to get everything down in his notebook. Closely he examined the tiny figurines placed on the walls of the houses; and the necklaces, like airy, silken wires, intricately woven, about the pale green necks of the Mushroom People. On the fingers of the women were many rings, and there were bracelets on their arms.

"All gold!" Horatio shouted over to Chuck and David. "And their cooking pots, and their dishes — gold! gold! gold!"

At this Ta put back his head and shouted with laughter.

"I think his ride in the creature of silver has been too much for him," he said. "His thoughts have been touched. But now come, my friends, and see how royally Mrs. Pennyfeather lives."

Once more Chuck and David picked up the chicken coop and were about to follow Ta, when they saw Horatio talking excitedly to a little group of Mushroom People who were gesturing up toward the mountains. When David looked back again, Horatio had disappeared, but at sight of Mrs. Pennyfeather in her new home, he was too excited to wonder where Horatio had gone.

Inside a fence of golden mesh, Mrs. Pennyfeather had a house almost as large and fine as Ta's. And in the fence were stuck all kinds of strange blooms, thick, waxy, succulent flowers of the palest colors, as though the Mushroom People had brought them and put them there as a sign of thanks to Mrs. Pennyfeather. David was about to call out to her (she was not to be seen, so she must have been having a nap inside her house), when Ta opened the gate and suggested they put her husband and children inside, and then call.

John, looking extremely ruffled and sulky, stood where he was put as though, after what *he'd* been through, he did not intend lifting a claw for anyone. But the young cockerel and the pullets, free at last, ran clucking and squawking all about as though they hadn't a brain in their silly heads, and at once Mrs. Pennyfeather appeared at the door of her

113

house. She simply stood there, gawking, paralyzed with astonishment.

"Mrs. Pennyfeather! Mrs. Pennyfeather!" cried David, running towards her. He picked her up, and she allowed herself to be patted and hugged and made over, all the while uttering little happy cries that sounded like "Qua-a-a, qua-qua-a-a!" Then, when her children gathered around the boys' legs, she struggled to be free. She gave each of the children a little poke with her beak, then hastened eagerly over to John. Round and round him she went, ducking her head and cooing to him — the foolish woman! And John never moved. He was deeply, deeply offended and apparently intended to make his wife suffer for it.

"Oh, that John!" exclaimed Chuck disgustedly. "What the heck a sensible creature like Mrs. Pennyfeather sees in him, I don't know."

"Well, he's a very fine, handsome —" began David, when all at once he turned, his attention caught by a growing murmur of angry shouts and cries.

"Look, Chuck, look!"

Outside Mrs. Pennyfeather's enclosure, Basidiumites were gathering round Ta and Mr. Theo, and they were all excited and making violent gestures.

When the boys reached the edge of the crowd,

they heard Ta demand sternly, *"Where has he gone?"* At once David knew Ta meant Horatio.

"He asked us about the stones of your necklace, Great Ta," spoke up a little Basidiumite. "And we told him they came from the Hall of the Ancient Ones high in the mountains."

"We told him the Hall was sacred," cried another. "We told him we took all our Silent Ones there."

Their Silent Ones, thought David. Could he mean — could he mean the dead?

"If he has been told all this, then," said Mr. Theo gravely, "I am afraid that Horatio Q. Peabody is already on his way."

"But he won't find what he seeks," exclaimed Ta. "Our Hall is high and deep. It is dangerous to reach, and may not be entered by strangers going alone."

"He has frightened us," cried the little Basidiumite who had spoken first. "He has said words to us which we don't understand."

"He said he could put our voices into a small box and make the voices be heard from the box anywhere without our going with it to speak. And he said that he could bring the forked lightning down out of the skies to do our work for us!"

The Mushroom People all shuddered with amazement.

"He said he could take earth and air and water and put them together and make something new. And he said he could take the air we breathe and split it up into tiny pieces so suddenly that they would fly apart with a huge and awful noise."

I guess he means he could make some kind of bomb, thought David.

The Mushroom People shuddered with horror.

"Why would he wish to do this frightful thing?"

"But worst of all," cried another Basidiumite, "he put a long white thing in his mouth. Then he took something out of his garment, a kind of small shiny box, and a flame came up out of this shiny box which he put to the end of the long white thing, and then he breathed great clouds of smoke out of his nostrils in two angry shoots, and the end of the white thing glowed like a fiery eye! And then — oh, and then he suddenly put back his head and began sending the smoke out of his mouth in circles which got larger and larger — and they came winding toward us, reaching for us — the big wavering gray rings that broke and stretched out; and we had to back away — to run away — or they would have clutched us and swallowed us! Oh, it was terrible;

116

he is an evil one, to breathe smoke. No good living thing can breathe smoke!"

"Why did you bring him here?"

The little Mushroom People were all turning and fixing their huge, luminous brown eyes on Chuck and David, and suddenly David felt his arms grow cold and his heart began to thump with fright. The little faces were no longer wreathed with smiles of welcome nor beaming with friendliness. The expressions of warmth and welcome were all gone — worst of all, it seemed to David, there were no expressions, none at all. One could not tell what these small unheard-of people had in their minds. For a moment the silence was terrifying, so terrifying that David could hear Chuck's breathing getting quick and hard, and then he felt Chuck's hand gripping his arm.

"We must go after this person at once," ordered Ta in a loud voice. "You, Mr. Theo, and you, Chuck and David, for you have brought him here and you must take him away. I shall pray that he does not arrive at the Hall of the Ancient Ones alone, even though he seems to speak and act like a mad person. Surely he is mad, for why else would he look and then scribble, look and scribble?"

"But he only wants to be able to tell the People

of the Great Protector what your planet is like," explained David desperately to Ta and the Basidiumites gathered about. "He's afraid he might forget something unless he writes it all down. He won't harm you, or steal anything, he only wants not to forget."

"*Make* him forget!" came a loud cry.

"Yes, make him forget! *He must forget everything!*" cried all the Basidiumites together.

"*Find him — take him away . . .*"

Now, as though a storm wind had blown across these strange little people, they all seemed taken with a fury together, and they began surging about this way and that so that David had no idea what to do nor where to turn. He could scarcely breathe for fright and when he caught a glimpse of Chuck's face, it was white.

Perhaps they are going to kill us, flashed into David's head. Perhaps we are going to die here on Basidium and never get back to earth nor see Mother and Dad again and Cap'n Tom and all our friends. And then he felt Ta's firm hand on his shoulder.

"Hurry!" ordered Ta in a low voice. "This way." Urgently he pushed Chuck and David through the crowd to the door of his palace and in they went and sped along through one silent room after another. Behind them hurried Mr. Theo, his tall hat firm on his head and his cloak flying out behind him. From far off the cries and furious shouts of the little green people could still be heard.

"But you are safe at any rate," remarked Ta as they emerged into an open glade of slender, delicate mushroom plants beyond which rose the mountains. "If you had stayed, I could not have answered for your lives. It is impossible to explain anything to those who are both angry and terrified."

CHAPTER 13

The Hall of
the Ancient Ones

So once more they set out into the mountains, not by the path they had taken on their first trip to Basidium when they had gone in search of the Place of Hidden Water, but in the opposite direction. Up and up they went, and as they climbed David saw one thing after another he remembered from the first time — birds, for instance, like small jeweled lizards, flying serpents with scales of luminous colors which flashed and glistened in the silver-green light. Those were lalas, Ta called out to them. And they had glimpses of great insects with whirring wings that skimmed past their ears. They thought they saw the morunbend again, the great slothlike creature they had seen on their other trip to Basidium; but nothing, no bird or insect or animal, stayed to be watched. All was vanishing, mysterious, half-seen, in the winding mists of the little planet. There were sounds, long, strange trills and flutings, and now and then a coughing and grunting from deep in the undergrowth.

"That must be more morunbends!" whispered Chuck in David's ear. "Dave, what if they — what if lots of them came out and — and lumbered right over us?"

But just then they heard a cry, and they saw Ta pointing across a deep gulch ahead of them to a great mountain that rose ahead, the highest mountain of all. They stared, and in a patch of clearing mist they saw for a moment two tiny figures wending their way to the summit. And down below them, but on the same trail, followed Horatio!

"They are on their way to the Hall!" Ta called back. "They are going to ask for forgiveness and wisdom. But they are doomed to misfortune, for even now they are unwittingly showing the Stranger the way to our Sacred Place."

Down, down they went into the gulch. Then in a surprisingly short time, considering what had looked to be the enormous distance between themselves and the two little figures of Mebe and Oru, the boys saw looming ahead of them a huge, cavernous maw in the side of the mountain. Mebe and Oru and

Horatio had disappeared. Inside the great darkness, which seemed to stretch away without end, it was like the entrance to a cathedral, echoing and cold.

"If the Stranger has entered here without asking permission of the Ancient Ones, which of course he would not think to do, all will go badly with him," said Ta in a low voice.

Now Ta raised his arms high, palms outward.

"May we enter, O Ancient Ones?" he cried. "We come to seek our kinsmen and to do honor to the Visitor you have sent among us. May we enter?"

The Visitor? Chuck and David asked one another with questioning looks. Surely, wondered David, Ta could not possibly mean Horatio. Who, then? Mr. Theo, perhaps? But somehow he felt that Ta meant someone else, yet he could not imagine who. Then, even as he stood wondering, there came what sounded like sighing, faraway voices. Echoes, they could have been, or the sighing of the winds in the enormous upper reaches of the cavern. Yet these sounds were different, more lingering, whispering, ghostly. David listened, and the hairs rose along the backs of his arms. Ta turned.

"We may enter. Come!"

Now he went to the side of the entranceway and

lighted two torches, one of which he gave to Mr. Theo, who held it aloft in his white-gloved hand.

Through the long, tortuous cavern they wound, deep into the mountain. After a while they came to a long room which opened off to one side, and at the opening the two boys stopped and stared, unable to believe what they saw. For here many, many little Basidiumites sat about, no longer green but waxy pale, peaceful and still as though they were asleep, or thinking, their eyes closed.

"This is the Place of Stillness," explained Ta to Mr. Theo and the boys. "When the breath goes from an old person, he is brought here, and there is a ceremony of singing and speaking of poems. And a strange thing," continued Ta, "is that when one returns to the Place of Stillness later, the old person who has been brought here is no longer wrinkled and aged but looks quite young again. So all the Silent Ones look young and peaceful." And indeed they all did.

Now Ta led on, and presently they came to what must have been the Central Hall. It was enormously high, the ceiling lost in darkness and shadow, and the walls were all covered with richly colored stones like those in Ta's necklace. A faint light came from

from there came voices — voices which to the boys were wonderfully familiar.

"Mebe and Oru!" cried Chuck.

"And someone else, Chuck! *Listen!*" Chuck listened, his eyes widening in unbelief. Across Mr. Theo's face crept an expression of incredulous surprise, while Ta stood there smiling as though he himself, somehow, had performed a miracle for their benefit.

"It's — but it *can't* be!" shouted Chuck.

But it could be — and it was —

"Mr. Bass!" called out David joyfully. "Tyco Bass! Tyco Bass! Where've you come from?" Eagerly he and Chuck raced forward to that little group at the far end of the hall, with Mr. Theo hastening after, his cape flapping, his tall hat tilting farther than ever over one eye and the flame of his torch streaming out behind.

Mebe and Oru were jumping about like a pair of excited rabbits at sight of their two friends from the Great Protector, and at the same time Tyco Bass stepped down from his chair to meet them, his hands stretched out in welcome.

"Oh, Mr. Bass — Mr. Bass — it *can't* be you! How can you be here? Where --"

"Where've you been?"

"You haven't changed a bit —"

"Why, you still have your gray gardening coat on —"

"And your old-fashioned boots —"

So he had, and the few fine hairs on his great, round, bald head lifted gently in a faint breeze as he came toward them; his little wizened face was wreathed in smiles, and his touch was, just as they remembered, like a breath of air. *Would* he float away?

"Mr. Bass, we built another space ship from your scribbles, I mean your notes, along with Mr. Theo —"

"Here's Mr. Theo —"

"You didn't expect to see *him,* did you, Mr. Bass — ?"

How excited everyone was! The boys gave little Mebe and Oru a good hug apiece, and Ta was overjoyed to know that his two foolish Wise Men were safe and sound and ready to come home again. Mr. Theo and Mr. Bass flung their arms around each other's necks and in the hubbub Mr. Theo's gloves were trampled underfoot and his hat fell off, collapsed flat, and rolled away like a hoop. How everyone talked, all at once, so that it was practically impossible to know just what anyone was saying.

But it didn't matter a bit — nobody cared, really; and then after a while they all grew calmer and settled down. Ta graciously offered Mr. Bass the seat of honor, then he himself took a large stone chair to the right of his guest. Everyone else sat round in a circle a little lower down.

"Mr. Bass — where've you been? Do tell us!"

"We miss you so much —"

"Aren't you *ever* coming back?"

"Won't we *ever* see you again?"

Mr. Bass put back his head and laughed with delight, as though the very sound of the boys' questions, tripping each other up, eager, impatient, affectionate, was something he had missed a great deal and had been wanting to hear once more.

"My young friends," he said, "if I were to tell you everything that has happened to me since I left earth on the storm wind, I would not know where to begin." At his words, "my young friends," spoken so warmly, the boys again felt that sense of electric excitement they'd known when they first talked to Mr. Bass in his little mushroom-shaped house on Thallo Street. "Speaking of travels, my dear Theo," he went on — "Oh, but there's no time — no time. At any rate, the Ancient Ones decreed that before I should settle in my new home on a planet in the solar system of another sun, I should be allowed a time of visiting.

"So I went about to all the places I had wanted to see in our own system: The rings of Saturn are breath-taking, seen close up, and there is a little planetoid amazingly like Basidium, which I call Lunaris, not far from the moon. What an unforgettable view it gives of the moon's surface! Needless to say, I saved the best for the last, a visit to my ancient homeland."

"Yes, Tyco arrived early this morning," put in Ta, "with the glad news that the creature of silver would be coming on this day. Thus, I was doubly happy. And thus I knew that I should go out to meet it at the place and time it had first landed. When you disappeared, Tyco, I was sure you had come here to the Hall of the Ancient Ones, but I must say I never guessed that Mebe and Oru —" Ta's words were cut off as though he had been struck.

For there came at this moment a cry from the direction of the Place of Stillness. A moment later Horatio dashed into the great Central Hall, his notebook clasped in one hand and a torch held high in the other. His eyes were wide and his face was shining with perspiration.

"Those people in there — they looked at me without moving or speaking — hundreds of them — who are they?" And he started to come forward when all at once, in spite of his fright, his eyes took in the beauty of the cavern walls pulsing with color in the rising and falling light of the torches. "The jewels of Basidium!" he breathed and he went closer and stared in wonder, his mouth hanging open. "Fantastic — unbelievable — enough to make possible a thousand scientific expeditions!"

At this, both Chuck and David started up, but Tyco Bass held out a restraining hand and shook his head at them in silence. Now Horatio turned and came slowly toward the little group. David got up.

"This is Professor Horatio Q. Peabody, Mr. Bass. He stowed away in our space ship and has been taking notes on Basidium ever since he got here. Professor Peabody, this is Mr. Tyco Bass."

"But I thought you — I thought that you — how did *you* arrive?" Horatio seemed absolutely thunderstruck.

Mr. Bass chuckled.

"I know now, Professor Peabody, that even travel in space ships is slow. You would not believe how quickly I came to Basidium once I had decided I must see it again. But we have so little time, before you and the boys must leave for earth, let us get on with our conversation. Do you remember that bottle of Basidium air you brought me, Chuck and David? I have been meaning to —"

"If we have so little time," broke in Horatio in that abrupt, rude fashion of his, shoving the torch into a holder and beginning to pace up and down, "I have something to say to you, Mr. Tyco Bass. No one, not an astronomer and a scientist, can imagine my state of mind during these past hours. My brain has reeled, it is true, yet I have kept one thing in the forefront of my thoughts. Surely you must realize that all facts concerning Basidium (most of which I now have in my notebook) belong, not to us, but to the world and must be given immediately to the world.

"What right had you to keep it a secret all this time? What kind of scientist are you? But I warn you, Basidium already belongs to the people of earth. I shall use my notes — I shall write a *great* paper, one that will be remembered forever — and you will learn that a single man can never stand in the way of knowledge."

Ta was gazing at Horatio sternly, but little Mebe and Oru listened in bewilderment. They seemed to have no idea at all what Horatio was talking about. Mr. Theo listened with the oddest expression on his face, and it was only when he winked quickly and secretly at the two boys that they were kept from speaking their anger and indignation. Mr. Bass watched Horatio with a curious little half-smile, and seemed in no way troubled by his furious outburst.

"You mean then, Mr. Peabody," remarked Mr. Theo when the other had finished, "that you would be quite willing for all kinds of men to come here and trample the face of Basidium, making a public place of it and breaking these peaceful lives and changing everything forever? I said little on the journey here, because I thought that perhaps the sight of these innocent Mushroom People might change your mind. But I see that it hasn't. And I can only say that I feel you are wrong, very wrong, to be determined to force events ahead so quickly."

"Yes," agreed Mr. Bass. "You *are* wrong, Mr. Peabody. Therefore, for your own good I am afraid that you must be forbidden ever to set foot on Basidium again."

At these words Horatio let out a kind of hoarse bark which was no doubt meant to be laughter.

"Who are you to forbid me anything? Why, I defy you!"

"Alas," replied little Mr. Bass, spreading his hands. "It would not be *me* you'd be defying, but the ancient Laws of Order, which nothing nor anyone in the universe can ever get round or escape in any way."

"What are they, Mr. Bass?" asked David.

"Those, David and Chuck, are the laws which decree that everything shall happen in its own way and in its own good time. He who insists on trying to break these laws works his own destruction."

"Then do you mean that Professor Peabody will be destroyed?"

"I don't know. But there are many ways of rendering helpless a breaker of the law other than by destroying him."

Now Horatio put back his head and laughed so loudly that the echoes of his laughter sounded wildly through the great hall.

"Then, my friends, I assure you I am willing to run the risk of being 'rendered helpless,' as Mr. Bass so nicely puts it. After all, I am not thinking of myself."

"Indeed, no," agreed Mr. Theo softly. "Nor are you thinking of fame and immortality, I suppose, but only of the people of earth. I must say you are a courageous man!"

"No one can deny that," nodded Mr. Bass. "And now I feel that it is time, David and Chuck, for you and Mr. Peabody to be starting back for the space ship. Otherwise you will be late."

"*Late!*" echoed Horatio suddenly in the strangest voice imaginable. "*Late*, you say!" And he turned and picked up his torch and stuffed his notebook into his pocket, gave them all one last, long piercing glance and strode away, disappearing round a turn a little way beyond, made by a great, outjutting rock.

Not two minutes later it was as though Basidium itself were coming to an end.

CHAPTER 14

The Anger of
the Ancient Ones

Surely the mountain had fallen in on them, and they were all crushed to death. Yet when David regained his senses, he knew that he was not hurt, only that he was in complete darkness and that it was not rock that was crushing him but thunder — such roaring, blasting, deafening thunder as he had never thought to hear in his whole life. He could only crouch, folded in upon himself, hoping numbly that the thunder would stop, for his eardrums ached with it, his head, his whole body ached, was smashed flat by it. Dimly he remembered that storm in which he and Chuck had been caught when they returned from Basidium the first time. Thunderbolts had rolled down the sky and crashed like cannon balls around the space ship and he had wondered then if it was to be the end. But that storm had

133

been nothing. For now the mountain was caving in. This thunder was the roar of tons of breaking rock. Some gigantic boulder would fall — any moment — in the next split second — and he would not know or feel anything ever again.

But the boulder did not fall. Even, for the space of a breath, there was silence. The thunder stopped. Then briefly, but not so loudly, it continued, stopped; there was another crash or two, and then stillness. No voice. No breath. David pricked his ears until they hurt in the effort to hear someone breathing. Perhaps they are all dead, he thought, and I am alone deep in this mountain on Basidium.

Then someone spoke, and it was Ta.

"The Ancient Ones are angry," he said in a low, ominous voice. "They have struck at us. They have closed the hallway with stone so that we cannot go out into the light again. They have blown out our torches so that we cannot see. They are angry because the Stranger came into their sacred place. We have come to an end."

Once more there was silence. Then there came another voice, and it was Mr. Bass's. How good it sounded! David thought he had never in his life heard anything so good and warm and comforting as the sound of Tyco Bass's voice.

"I don't believe They're angry at us, Great Ta," said Tyco calmly. "We have done nothing. It was the fault of no one here that Horatio Q. Peabody stowed away on the space ship. It was the fault of no one here that he found his way to the Hall of the Ancient Ones, or that he did not know enough to ask permission to enter. Perhaps They are angry at Horatio Peabody and have made an end of him, but I believe that we shall get out. First of all, are we all here?"

"I don't know," piped up little Mebe. "How could we be? After all that thunder, and the mountain falling, it stands to reason we are dead."

"Well, I'm still alive, and I'm here," came a shaken voice which was Chuck's.

"Me, too," David managed to get out, but he didn't at all like the tone of his own voice, which did not sound nearly as firm and courageous as he had tried to make it.

"I'm here, Tyco," announced Mr. Theo as pleasantly as though he were sitting in an ice-cream parlor having a sundae. "But I must say that in all my wanderings, through steaming undergrowths to the bitterest mountain heights, I have never undergone such a shattering experience."

"Dear me! Dear me!" exclaimed Mr. Bass, who, even so, did not sound greatly disturbed. "Now, let me think. First, we must light the torches again. We can breathe, so I imagine they will burn, as both living things and fire need air."

Now there came a rustling as Ta felt about for their torches, and then a scraping as he worked his flints, which he carried deep in a pocket inside his robe. In a moment, there were sparks, then the torch flared up, and in another moment both Mr. Theo's torch and those of Mebe and Oru had been lighted. What a comforting sight it is after danger, thought David, to see other faces like one's own, or even a little like one's own.

They looked about and saw that the part of the Hall in which they stood was untouched. But beyond them, where the great boulder had jutted out, there was no longer any opening, only a solid wall of tumbled rock studded with huge jagged chunks of those same richly colored stones that encrusted the walls of the cavern.

"What wouldn't Horatio Peabody give to carry away one of those jewels of Basidium, as he calls them," murmured Mr. Theo.

"Perhaps he has given his life," said Ta.

"And maybe ours too," added Chuck bitterly. "This is all his fault. Look at that. We'll never get out of here!"

"Oh, come now," comforted Mr. Bass. "I think we are not going to suffer any immediate finish. In the days of my ancestors there was the legend of another, secret passageway into this part of the Sacred Hall. And generations ago, I was taken through it by my grandfather. I *wonder* —"

"But there is not so much as a thumb's-width of space in all the walls of this place — not a crack that even a tiny lala could creep through," stated Ta, and he swept his arm about on a level with his shoulder.

"No, Great Ta," assented Mr. Bass, "not hereabouts" — and he too held his arm out as Ta had done. "But it remains in my memory that I was told, 'In the most high place —' and that is all. I remember it had something to do with the great throne, there where you sit during the ceremonies. Therefore we shall start behind your throne. And we shall continue upward to this most high place, which to all eyes, during untold time, has remained curtained in darkness. Come. We are going to have to cling for our lives while we search for that opening which I am certain is up there."

And so, after Mr. Theo had recovered his opera hat and clapped it firmly on his head, and his gloves, which he put in his pocket, they gathered behind the throne and started climbing. Straight up they crept, finding foothold wherever they might, and whoever was in difficulty passed his torch momentarily to the person below. For they could not possibly have found their way up without light. And at last, when David thought he could not have wriggled his way up another inch, he heard Mr. Bass give a cry of joy and, looking up, he saw the little man's face peering at them, wreathed in smiles, from what appeared to be nothing more than a blotch of shadow.

Then he disappeared. After him went Ta, then Mr. Theo, then little Mebe and Oru, squeaking with terror lest they should slip, then the two boys.

Once inside the passage that opened before them, however, David noticed as they went along that the way became narrower and narrower. At turnings, where clefts in the huge and timeless rock created two pathways, one leading to the right and one to the left, Mr. Bass would pause. And in these intervals it seemed to David his heart thudded so loudly he wondered the sound of it didn't reverberate like a drumbeat against the walls of the labyrinth. Then on they would go again, sometimes shinnying up the bare face of a high step, or climbing down over a steep and sudden drop.

And as they made their way through the mountain, the sides of the passage drew steadily in until there was scarcely room for their bodies to pass without shoulders touching rock. Then at last, as they made another turning, David saw by the light of the torches whose flames flared and faded and flared again like live things, that the cleft in the rock was now so narrow that they would have to go sideways.

We'll never make it, he told himself in despair. The cleft will get narrower and narrower until there is no least crack left. It's hopeless. . . . "Hopeless," he whispered to Chuck when he turned his face to the side to squeeze through.

Chuck could only nod, and David saw his face was scratched and dirty and glistening with perspiration.

"We should never have come, Dave," he got out finally. "We were fools to come."

But at this moment words flashed into David's

mind like an answer. In his memory he heard Mr Bass speaking. "You mustn't doubt, David. Remember that, *you are never to doubt.*" Yes, it was what Mr. Bass had told them before they set out for Basidium the first time. And despite everything, they'd got home safely, hadn't they?

It was very strange. David and Chuck could now scarcely force their way along, but it was as though Mr. Bass and Mr. Theo and Ta and the little Wise Men were compressible. Perhaps it's because they're soft inside like mushrooms, thought David. It must be they have no bones, being spore people and not human.

"No bones — that's it," he whispered, and just as he said it, there was a shout ahead.

"We're out, boys," came Mr. Theo's voice. "Come along quickly, we're out!"

With shrill, small cries like excited mice, little Mebe and Oru somehow managed to scuttle past the boys' legs. They drew in upon themselves and immediately disappeared through a crevice from which actually came the soft, silvery gleam of late Basidium day.

"But we can't make it, Mr. Theo," cried Chuck in the darkness behind David, and his voice shook with disappointment and fright. "Tell Mr. Bass we're too big. Tell him it's hopeless. We just can't squeeze through."

"We've got bones, Mr. Bass," yelled David, trying desperately to insert himself into the narrow space. "We're stuck. We're not compressible like you." His eyes burned and his throat ached horribly. He wondered if Chuck, too, could be wanting to cry. What a darned, stupid baby, he told himself furiously, but his eyes continued to burn and he thought suddenly, queerly of that beautiful big chocolate cake his mother had made for them and which hadn't even been touched yet. They'd never eat it now, that was a certain thing.

But there seemed to be some sort of conference going on outside, for the boys could hear little Mebe and Oru chirping back and forth with such eagerness they sounded like two crickets. David got down on his knees so as to get a good look at the outside world, and there was Mr. Bass nodding, and Ta seeming to give an order, and then Mebe and Oru ran over to a clump of low growth. Presently it was plain they had undressed, for their robes were now flung over. Puzzled, David saw Mr. Bass pick them up and come across to the face of the rock.

"What is it, Dave — what is it? Tell me!" panted Chuck eagerly. "What's going on?"

"They want us to get out of our clothes, I think."

"Now, boys," said Mr. Bass, standing at the crevice and smiling in at them encouragingly, "you must put on these robes which are as slick and thin as paper and which will allow you to slide past the rock quite easily. The material is tough too, so that it won't tear. Mebe and Oru are quite right. Your own clothes are far too thick and bundlesome — they're all that keep you back. You will see. Hurry now! You're quite safe. Never fear."

Sure enough — in a trice the boys, in their borrowed garments, had popped through the crevice like squirted seeds.

CHAPTER 15

The Triumph of Horatio

NEVER FEAR! *Never fear,* little Mr. Bass had said. They were almost at the city of the Mushroom People again, but Mr. Bass was gone.

"The best of good fortune on your homeward journey, boys," he had cried, holding out his long thin hands to them, one to each. "And tell Professor Peabody, if you should find him, that he must think twice about making public that great scientific paper of his. Cousin Theo is right, you know. We can't hurry things!" Now Tyco Bass smiled, his whole small wizened face lighting up, and his large eyes shining. Chuck and David held tightly to his hands as though to keep him from disappearing into thin air, or from simply floating away. "Good-by for the present, Theo. I must say you are looking amazingly spry for your age. Remarkably well preserved you are — and still such a fashion plate. Top hat and white gloves still on after all we've been through! Now remember, Mebe and Oru, a little confidence in yourselves is all you need. Farewell, Great Ta. It has been a deep pleasure to me to see you again. I knew your great-great-great-great grandfather well — a fine man he was."

Then lightly Mr. Bass had walked away. He was there, and then suddenly he just was not. Nothing was heard but the sigh of the wind, a soft, perpetual whispering in the shadowy heights of the rock.

"Was he really here?" David asked of them all. But no one answered.

Now they were just above the city which lay in a little valley ahead. How pleased and proud Mebe and Oru were, skipping about all the way down the mountain and telling the story over and over again of how it had been *their* idea entirely that Chuck and David could not escape the rock until they, too, had on nothing but the robes of the bilba tree. Now the two little Wise Men were back in their own clothes again and Chuck and David had on their jeans and shirts and leather jackets, which plainly Mebe and Oru thought dreadfully ugly.

"How can you move at all?" they asked in wonderment. "What thick, rough, strange things to want to put on your bodies."

Ta and Mr. Theo were speaking of Horatio.

"Do you remember," remarked Mr. Theo, "how he cried, '*Late!*' in such a peculiar voice just as he left us in the Central Hall? What could he have meant? What do you suppose he had in mind?"

"Perhaps," replied Ta ominously, "he meant that he himself would be more than late, for he never intended to return to the space ship at all, but to remain on Basidium for a time."

"Or perhaps he meant," added Chuck, "that *we'd* be more than late, because he never intended *us* to get back to the ship!"

"My gosh, Chuck, you mean *he* caused the rock slide in the mountain so we couldn't get out, and so he could stay here as long as he liked and take the space ship back *himself?*"

"Dear me," murmured Mr. Theo, "what a dreadful thought. I could not think so badly of him as that."

"No, Chuck," David said, after cogitating for a moment, "I believe Horatio's foolish, but not wicked. I don't think he'd want to take our lives."

"And I believe," said Ta, "that your foolish one could not have dislodged so great a rock as to cause the inner cavern to crumble. I think as I first thought, that it was the anger of the Ancient Ones, and that your Stranger no longer exists."

"Hello there," came a shrill, harsh voice at this instant. "I say — hello there!"

Stunned with amazement, the whole group came to a standstill, for there, racing down an incline a little way off to the left, came Horatio. His clothing was torn, his face was scratched and bloody, and he looked as though he had been to the Underworld and back, which of course he had — in a manner of speaking. But what was hardest of all to believe was that in one hand he still carried his everlasting note-book, and now he waved it at them in triumph!

"Lost!" he got out in a sort of croak as he staggered up to them. "Lost! Almost done for! The mountain, you know — thought I'd never get out. Got all turned around in that awful place with those rows and rows of Basidiumites in it, everyone silent and staring at me. Almost went mad! But look here!" And from his pocket he took pieces of stone like those which encrusted the Great Hall. "Just made it by the skin of my teeth. Rock slide — right behind me. Whole contraption fell in —

146

rocks crashing all around me — how I made it, I'll never know. Charmed life, that's what I have. And look! The jewels of Basidium! Oh, wait'll Dr. Frobisher sees these!" crowed Horatio. "How his eyes'll bug out. He'll *have* to believe, and all those pals of his who never look at me, never notice me, never suppose for a moment I've a brain in my head! I'll show 'em — I'll tell 'em. Wait'll they read my paper — and then these jewels to prove everything I say, to back everything up to the hilt!"

And suddenly Horatio lifted his head and let out such a peal of harsh laughter that David wondered if his narrow escape hadn't sent the poor man right out of his mind.

"Take it easy, Professor Peabody," he exclaimed. "You ought to —"

"And such things I've written," Horatio went on, paying no attention to anyone. "I've finally pinned it all down. These people here are like a very ancient earth people, with their jewelry of fine, gold wire, and their songs and poetry and dancing. And yet the plant life and animal life are somewhat like that of the still more ancient Age of Reptiles, except of course that nothing here is huge except the mushrooms and that thing called a morunbend. An incredible combination — simply *incredible!*"

But Mr. Theo was slowly shaking his head.

"No, Mr. Peabody, it isn't Basidium that's incredible, it's you! However, you cannot keep those jewels. They're not yours, you see."

"Let him keep them," said Ta calmly. "It doesn't matter at all — not now."

Not now — *not now!* What, wondered David, could Ta possibly mean by that?

Back in the little city, the Mushroom People were all out waiting for them, their rage spent, and smiles of welcome once more lighting their small green faces. Whether they had forgotten why they were angry, or whether it was the fact that Horatio was once more in Ta's keeping, David could not imagine. But at any rate, all seemed peaceful and happy once more.

Now Ta went into his dwelling place and motioned Horatio, the boys and Mr. Theo and his Wise Men to follow. Outside, the Basidiumites gathered around the entranceway.

"You will now get The Drink, Mebe and Oru," ordered Ta.

At this, the eyes of the little Wise Men opened wide in wonder.

"They are amazed, my friends, because The Drink is so seldom brought forth. It is rare and difficult to make, and the way of its making has been handed down to us from ancient times. It is always for one person alone. Such a person, worthy of The Drink, rarely comes to us — he is hard to find."

There was a deep silence as Mebe and Oru left. When they returned, one carried a tall, beautifully wrought goblet of pure gold and the other a small round cask which looked as if it had been made from the dried and highly polished trunk of a young mushroom tree. Now, still in utter silence, some of the contents of the cask was poured into the goblet.

Now Ta held out the goblet in both hands. He did not look at anyone, but away over their heads.

"For him who has come so unexpectedly among us," spoke Ta in a low, vibrant voice. "For him who is adventurous and courageous, capable of many wonders, whose imagination sees into the future, whose mind is like the Shining One in the sky that lights all it touches and leaves nothing the same thereafter. For him whom nothing can daunt, who has no fear of any kind. For him, and him alone, is this Drink brewed."

And because of the vibrancy and darkness of Ta's

voice, something, some hidden meaning in it which he could not read, caused a chill of terror to go down David's spine. He felt the hairs lift along the backs of his arms.

Then all the Basidiumites standing beyond the entranceway raised their voices in song, the flutes sounded, and Ta lifted high the goblet, extending it to — Mr. Theo surely, cried David to himself, for was not Mr. Theo courageous and imaginative? Hadn't he made the space ship go? Hadn't he traveled without fear over all the world, through wind and storm and heat and cold, through the most extreme dangers?

But horror of horrors! Horatio Q. Peabody, without a moment's hesitation, reached out his hands with an expression of blind self-satisfaction and self-gratification. Never for a moment had he doubted The Drink was for him! He smiled eagerly, his eyes upon the goblet, his face lighted with triumph. And this open display of vanity and egotism was so terrible to behold that David could not bear it and had to look away, to stare down at his hands, his face scarlet with embarrassment. But Ta, strangely enough, allowed Horatio to take The Drink without protest, though on his face there was a frightening gravity.

150

At last, when David looked up again, he saw that Horatio had drained the cup. There was not a drop left. Now Horatio set it down and looked about proudly.

"Great Ta," he cried, "I am humbly grateful that this honor has been bestowed upon me. And I promise you that you shall not regret having shown me your trust and faith. We shall push back the edges of ignorance. We shall make Basidium known to all, and prove Tyco Bass wrong. You have no idea of the wonders in store for you, nor of what these wonders can do. Why, this will be the history-making experiment of all time! Men shall speak of it a thousand years from now — and it shall begin when I return —" then he looked about very sternly and deeply at everyone gathered there — "for I *shall* return!"

Ta rose and smiled and nodded his head, and then Mebe and Oru smiled and nodded *their* heads. Now Ta beckoned everyone out and they started for the space ship, Ta and Horatio and Mr. Theo going on ahead.

Behind them, David and Chuck pulled the little Wise Men to one side, for there was something they had to say.

"We're so ashamed," David said. "We *knew* Ta

meant the drink for Mr. Theo as a kind of celebration that he'd decided to stay. *He's* the brave, courageous, imaginative one. *He's* gone through all sorts of dangers, and he was wise enough to understand Mr. Bass's notes on the making of space ships. But that Horatio Peabody just took it for granted The Drink was for him! It was *awful* — I can't tell you how ashamed we are!"

But amazingly enough, Mebe and Oru winked at each other and chuckled.

"It's all right, boys," said Mebe.

"The Great Ta meant everything to be just the way it was!" said Oru.

The boys stared at them, thunderstruck.

"Yes. You see," went on Mebe, "that was The Drink of Forgetfulness. Only once or twice in a lifetime is it necessary to give some misguided person this drink, usually someone very conceited, someone who thinks so highly of himself that when the Great Ta speaks just as he did now, the person is always absolutely sure The Drink is meant for him. The Ancient Ones have decreed that The Drink is never to be *forced* on the guilty person. But it is never necessary to force him to drink. Out of vanity and pride, he always takes it eagerly and drinks it all — every drop."

"The Drink of Forgetfulness — yes!" cried Chuck. "So that when he returns to earth, he'll forget Basidium and all his plans for bringing earth people here?"

"Pre-*cise*ly," beamed Mebe and Oru. Oh, they had indeed had a long talk with Mr. Bass in the Hall of the Ancient Ones! David, even now, could just hear Mr. Bass say, "Pre-*cise*ly!" — his favorite word.

At the space ship, Mr. Theo was already busy unloading the bags of grain, as well as the rest of his possessions, and Ta was sending the Mushroom People away because of the roar and flame of the take-off. However, many of the more brave and curious ones were seen to go only a little distance away and then peek out from behind the mushroom trees. Now once more there was a leavetaking, but this time the boys were having to say good-by to Mr. Theo, of whom they had grown so fond.

"Are you sure you want to stay behind, Mr. Theo?" wailed Chuck. "We'll miss you so much. Won't you and Mr. Bass *ever* come back?"

"I have a feeling, dear friends, that Tyco has much to do beyond the realm of our planets. But I know you will see him again sometime. And as for me," said Mr. Theo, smiling at them and plainly quite moved at their reluctance to leave him, "I have my work cut out for me here. But I still have Tyco's notes on the mysteries of space ships and I remember everything I did, so that perhaps — who knows? — I may once again knock at your door some still night, quite unexpectedly, just as I did not long ago. See, here is the box you asked me about when we started off. I filled it full of all sorts of chemicals and tools and odds and ends of things I thought I might find useful on Basidium."

"But perhaps you won't have to figure out the mysteries of space ships again, Mr. Theo — not if Horatio gets back here with this one!" Chuck reminded him.

But Mr. Theo laughed.

"Then watch," he said, "two hours from the time of his take-off, if you know of it, and I shall signal you. We will keep the space ship here, safe and sound, along with Horatio. He shall not go forward with any more of his plans, I assure you, for changing the face of Basidium!"

"Did you say you'd *signal* to us, Mr. Theo?" cried David.

"Dear me, yes — didn't I tell you? But of course, we've had no time to talk, really. Well, this is Tyco's lantern, you know"— and Mr. Theo held it up — the lantern he'd almost forgotten when they were about to take off and that Dr. Topman had rescued for him. "This is another of Tyco's inventions of which you boys have no real understanding: his marvelous light, his cellar light. It isn't like anything we know of. What is it, then? I've no idea. I only know this, that no man on earth would believe its power. What you have seen is only the faintest peep, the merest glimmering, glowworm peep. But turn it on to its fullest magnitude — as I intend doing should Horatio Peabody land on Basidium again — and it will signal to you, three long flashes and one short, across fifty thousand miles of space!"

"But that's im-*possible*, Mr. Theo —"

"Not at all, not at all. Nothing is impossible. You must remember that. Watch, and perhaps you will see that I tell you the truth. I shall also signal you should anything unusual take place or be about to take place. Be ready."

Now the boys bade good-by to Ta and little Mebe and Oru, took one last look at the elegant figure of Mr. Theo — who, oddly enough, fitted with absolute naturalness against the Basidium sky, despite his formal though rather battered costume — and were boosted up into the ship. Then Horatio, after a long stare at this lovely, unheard-of landscape, climbed up too, and they all leaned out waving and calling. The door was closed and bolted, the oxygen urn was turned on. David glanced out to see that every living thing was well away from the space ship, then he made a final, farewell gesture with his hand at the four standing waiting to see them go — turned on the rocket motor, and pulled back the stick.

There was the frightful glare of red together with that familiar terrifying roar and the wrenching jerk that seemed to tear them apart. When they recovered their senses, the boys turned and grinned at Horatio. But he was limp and white and almost unable to speak.

"This is one moment," he gasped, "that I shall never get used to, no matter how many trips I take back and forth to Basidium."

CHAPTER 16

In the Path of the Meteors

THE BOYS really felt rather sorry for Horatio. David had Mr. Theo's seat now, Chuck was in the middle where David had sat before, and Horatio was over near the door, writing feverishly as usual just as if, thought David, it were all going to amount to something. Poor old Horatio.

"I'll never get it all down," he cried. "There's so much and it's all somehow a confusion — I mean, what to put first! I thought I had everything, but now I keep thinking of things, the tiniest details, and yet I must capture them. I must capture it all, every last bit. Well, now I must keep calm, I must keep my thoughts orderly. First things first, I always say. Oh my, *what* will Dr. Frobisher think? Whom do you suppose he will wish to invite? For my lecture, I mean."

"So you have decided not to wait, then, Professor Peabody?"

"*Wait!* Impossible! But now, you know, I have been thinking. That name Basidium," Horatio continued, "really, that is not right. It simply won't do — sounds artificial, made up. Basidium, Basidium — no, not fitting, I think. Mushrooms, of course — Basidiomycetes — yet that is rather obvious, after all. It needs something more dignified. Let me see: one of the planets was first named after the astronomer who discovered it. Bass — Basidium — still, Tyco Bass has done little actual work in connection with it. And when one thinks of what I — oh, yes, one might say, rather, in view of the paper I shall publish on it — *Peabody's Planet!* Ah," breathed Horatio in delight. "And not for myself, but in the interests of euphony. *Peabody's Planet*. Oh, what an *ex*-cellent name!"

Chuck and David were absolutely choking with indignation.

"Yew-fimmy!" yelled Chuck, quite beside himself. "Who in heck's *he*, and what's *he* got to do with it?"

"Euphony, my dear boy," explained Horatio, rather amused, "means a combination of sounds pleasant to the ear."

"Pleasant to *your* ear, you mean!" shot back Chuck rudely, "You vain, pompous, blown-up old — old *thing!*" And he was about to light into Horatio good and proper when David suddenly grasped his arm so hard and tight that Chuck let out a sharp yelp of protest.

David, unaware of whether Chuck was looking or not, stared out into space — and what he saw made his tongue stick to the roof of his mouth so that he could not speak.

For there, rushing toward them through the blackness, was a swarm of meteors, almost invisible except that they were dimly, dimly lighted by the far-off blazing sun and thus made more ghostly than ever in their silent, onrushing flight. But then, just when David was about to cry out in horror that they would be stormed by the meteors as though by a hail of rocks which would pound the ship to pieces, he was further appalled to behold the meteors begin to whirl in a funnel-shaped circle. Then, as though caught in some giant whirlpool, in some fearsome, invisible maelstrom, they swept downward — the whole lot of them — *and completely vanished from sight!*

For what seemed an endless instant in time, Chuck and David remained frozen at the window

159

of the space ship, staring into blackness where once a cloud of meteors had sped toward them. Long since, of course, the place of their disappearance had been left behind. But the boys could not move. They could not believe what their eyes had told them. Then slowly David turned.

"Did you see it, Chuck?"

"Yes," answered Chuck in a low, shaken voice, "I saw it."

"They disappeared into it."

"Yes — they did."

"It was —"

"That's it — that's what it was: *the hole in space. And we saw it with our own eyes, both of us!*"

"Just as Mr. Bass said."

Again they were silent; then something dawned on David. What of Horatio? He twisted round, and there was Horatio busily scratching as usual, scratching, scratching, scratching into his little book.

"Professor Peabody, did you see — ?"

Horatio only frowned and looked up impatiently.

"See *what*, David?"

"Why, the hole in space. The meteors — they were rushing at us, a whole swarm, but they disappeared, right in front of our eyes! Chuck and I both saw!"

Horatio studied the two boys gravely, his lips pursed rather pityingly. Then he shook his head in amazement.

"*Tchk! Tchk!* It is quite unbelievable what the power of suggestion will do to the childish mind, especially when that suggestion comes from a source which the child reveres. Really, the whole thing is simply not worth discussing."

"But, Professor Peabody, it's true! I swear it's true! We saw —"

"Please," cut in Horatio, holding up his hand. "I don't wish to hear anything further about this preposterous business of a hole in a hole. I've a *great* deal to do before any more of the details which I wish to set down escape me." Then he looked at them angrily. "Already your interruption has cost me an *extremely* valuable deduction. I can't understand it. A moment ago I had an idea in my head — something which I had carefully pieced together because of what I saw on Basidium. But now it is gone. And — and besides that, other incidents, other facts which I *particularly* wished to note, seem to be drifting from me." He rubbed his hand over his eyes in bewilderment. "I am beginning to feel quite — quite *confused* — and it frightens me. I don't like it. For the love of goodness," he finished in

sharp annoyance, "let me alone. No more nonsense."
And once more he started in his furious scribbling
as though he were running a race against time.

David looked at Chuck — and Chuck at David.
Then silently Chuck made the motion of picking up
something hollow in both hands and drinking from
it, and David watched him and nodded in grave
agreement. Already, then, the Drink of Forgetfulness was beginning to work on Horatio.

CHAPTER 17

The Young Lady
Named Bright

W<small>HEN NEXT</small> David opened his eyes and looked out of the window of the space ship, he saw the earth — a huge globe suspended in nothingness and drifted over with fleecy wisps of dazzling white. He must have been asleep, otherwise he wouldn't have had to open his eyes and "come to." But why was it he never could remember the instant of falling asleep, or what he had been doing or thinking at the time? It was all very mysterious. At any rate, the rocket motor had cut off and the ship had turned round into free fall, so now David turned the motor on again so that they should land more lightly.

Suddenly Chuck stirred and rubbed his eyes and then leaned over to look out too.

"Why doesn't it just plunge downward?" he murmured. "The earth, I mean. There it hangs as though something held it up. Why doesn't it just drop down the way we're doing now?"

"But we're only dropping, Chuck, because the earth is pulling us. There's no *down* in space. Besides, the earth is spinning around the sun, and the gravity of the sun keeps it in that orbit."

"Yes, I know that, really. All the same, when you look at the earth the way we're doing now, not able to see any proof of its spinning, and there it is with space all round it — it just looks — well, I don't know — it's all awfully hard to believe. It's kind of a miracle."

"Look, do you suppose that's South America, and that deep blue the Pacific? It must be. And we'll go plunging down, and all because of Mr. Bass and Mr. Theo, we'll land, out of that whole globe, right on Cap'n Tom's beach. Do you suppose we'll ever see it again like this, Chuck? We've *got* to! How could we get along now without knowing we can hop into our space ship and look down on the earth like this — or see Basidium all pale green below us?"

"Well, why can't we do it whenever we like, Dave, as long as we stick to Mr. Bass's schedule? I don't see why not."

"I know — but —" and David gave a little nod

of his head in the direction of Horatio, sound asleep and snoring fit to wake the dead. "*Br-r-r-r,*" grated Horatio, his head fallen over on his chest, his pen slipped from his grasp, and his notebook (worse luck!) safely tucked away and making a bulge in his inside jacket pocket. "*B-r-r-r!*" and then suddenly, "Pawk!" It was so awful you wondered why he didn't scare himself out of his skin; but he must have been absolutely exhausted, because he looked to David as if he might sleep forever.

"Chuck, does it seem to you that it really happened?"

Chuck eyed him sharply for a second.

"You mean about the hole, don't you, Dave?"

"Yes. You know, maybe we dreamed it. It was the first thing I thought of when I woke up: that maybe we'd dreamed it."

"How come we both dreamed it, then? How come I knew what you were talking about just now, even though you didn't tell me what you meant?"

"I know. That's it. There's no argument, really. We both know what we know."

David was silent then, watching the earth draw closer and closer, not with alarming speed, but gradually, so that you were scarcely aware no matter how steadily you watched. "Shall we tell my mother and dad and Cap'n Tom? Would we have the nerve, Chuck?"

Chuck bit his lip and frowned deeply. Then he gave his verdict.

"We just can't. At least not right away. It's too — it's too — oh, no, Dave. We'll tell 'em about seeing Mr. Bass again, and about the Place of Stillness and the Hall of the Ancient Ones, and all that. But the hole in space — no. That'll have to wait until we can break it to them bit by bit. Of course, they won't believe us. They'll be polite, but they won't believe, and you can't blame 'em. We haven't any proof like we had of Basidium."

Each boy was lost in thought for a little, then David turned to Chuck and grinned.

"But it doesn't matter, does it, whether *anyone* believes us. We've got it in our heads. *We* can talk about it. Chuck, do you suppose the comets and meteors that plunged into that hole are lost forever? Do you suppose they just don't exist *anywhere?*"

"Well, don't you remember what Mr. Theo told us on the way down the mountain? They wouldn't exist where any physical eyes could see them in a physical way — because they're in *another dimension*. And they're going at the exact speed of light —"

"That's right — now I remember. What was the limerick Mr. Theo told us?

> There was a young lady named Bright
> Whose speed was far faster than light;
> She set out one day,
> In a relative way,
> And returned home the previous night.

"When a body travels *slower* than the speed of light —"

"Which is 186,000 miles a second," broke in Chuck.

"Yeah — well, when a person travels slower than that, the way we do, he can start from birth and grow gradually older —"

"But when he travels *faster* than the speed of light, the way the young lady named Bright did, then he'd go backwards in time, the way she did when she got home the previous night — only of course he wouldn't any longer be physical. He couldn't be. And if he were to travel at the *exact* speed of light, he'd stay forever'n forever'n forever the same. How *awful!*" Chuck finished, making an aghast face.

"Golly!"

"Golly what?" spoke up a muffled voice beside them. And they turned, and there was Horatio studying them groggily out of bloodshot, rheumy eyes.

"Golly-wog," said David.

Now Horatio passed his hand over his face and sat up rather unsteadily.

"I do feel peculiar!" he exclaimed. "As if I'd been hit over the head. How are we doing? Almost home?" Then he stretched a bit and looked out of the window. "Good heavens!" he gasped. "Good heavens, why, there it is!"

"Well, what would you have said if it *wasn't* there?" laughed David.

"I know, but — but it's quite a sight, isn't it?"

"Yes, it is. Quite a sight. And you'd better take a good look at it, Professor Peabody, because you may never see anything like it again."

At this, Horatio gave David a long, strange look.

"Whether I shall ever see it again or not has to do with me alone. *I* shall decide that." He seemed very calm and sure of himself, but all at once he frowned. "You know, it seems to me that we're speaking differently now — we are, of course, speaking English. Chair — table — for instance. C-h-a-i-r. That is English. But what was the Basidiumites' word for chair? I can't seem to recall."

Chuck groaned and David sighed.

"Neither can we, Professor Peabody. And it's no

use racking your brains to try to remember. But can you get back anything of the *way* they talked?"

A strained, anxious expression settled on Horatio Peabody's thin young face. He swallowed. Then he carefully and thoughtfully bit right round the nail of the first finger of his right hand.

"Well," he began, "well, let me see now. It seems — that it was something like Chinese. High, light, singsong. But far away — very — very — far away —"

"And their music, Professor Peabody, can you remember that? And what they called those instruments they played?"

Now the strained, anxious expression became almost distraught.

"Instruments?" he cried. "Instruments, you say?" And then his face changed; it positively shone with a look of blissful relief. "Doesn't matter!" he exclaimed, beaming and happy, taking his notebook from his pocket. "Doesn't matter if all this has escaped me — it's here safe and sound. The whole marvelous, fantastic business." He gazed on his notebook with love and tenderness. "You know, my friends, if I do say it myself, I think I did a tremendous job on my notes. I have really set down some *dizzying* facts and ideas." Radiating joy and anticipation, he slid the fat notebook back into his inside pocket and slapped it several times with beaming self-satisfaction.

David, watching him, felt his heart grow heavy. What difference did it make if the Drink of Forgetfulness had made him lose most of his memory of Basidium, whether it had confused him so that he would not, without help, be able to give his lecture or write that Scientific Paper of the Ages? There the whole thing still was in that darned notebook.

"Look, Dave, look! We're almost home!"

David leaned to look and there, far, far below, was Cap'n Tom's beach, a tiny strand of paleness between the dark, heaving expanse of the Pacific and the cypress-furred and rocky stretches of the Monterey coast. Now, as they came closer, it seemed to David he could detect small black specks on the paleness. Nearer, nearer they came — and there, at last, could be seen quite plainly the waving arms and excited movements of what must be his mother and father and Cap'n Tom. And then David stared round in astonishment.

For — would you believe it? — Horatio Q. Peabody, with the air of a homecoming conquerer, was leaning back in his seat and singing "California, Here I Come" at the top of his voice.

PART THREE

The Fall of Horatio

Hen-tracks

B<small>Y THE TIME</small> the ship had thudded upon the sand
and the door had been snatched open and the boys
had stumbled over Horatio and jumped into the
arms of Dr. Topman and Cap'n Tom, Horatio had
regained his usual dignity. Of course he too had to
leap and then to sprawl rather awkwardly, but all
the same he recovered himself quickly and the look
on his face said that he had everything well under
control.

But Mrs. Topman let out a sharp cry of annoyance.

"Good *heavens*, Professor Peabody, you can't
think what a lot of worry you've caused me! I simply couldn't *believe* you'd do a thing like that —
stow away in the boys' space ship — even though my
husband and Cap'n Tom swore up and down there

173

was simply no other way you could have disappeared. And then leaving your clothes in a lump like that under the blankets at Mr. Bass's! Really!"

Horatio Peabody smiled benignly as one determined to have patience with the little absurdities of women.

"Dear Mrs. Topman, it was most kind of you to be concerned as to my whereabouts. But in view of the circumstances — the discovery of a new satellite and all that the discovery would mean to astronomy — I did not very well see how I could refrain from going. There will be repercussions of this journey, repercussions that will be heard generations from now! Therefore, you can understand that I have much to do. Now, please, let us start back to the house at once so that I can pack and return as quickly as possible to the Frobishers'. I wish, of course, to talk everything over with the doctor before I make anything public."

For a second David's father and mother and Cap'n Tom just stood and looked at Horatio.

"I see," said Cap'n Tom at last, as though he were controlling himself with an effort. "I see — before *you* make anything public! But I understood that it was the wish of Mr. Tyco Bass that the discovery of Basidium was to remain secret — at least for the present."

"Yes," burst out David, "and Mr. Bass told us that anyone who broke the ancient Laws of Order could only come to destruction —"

"Mr. Bass was up on Basidium, Grandpop, and he told Professor Peabody —"

"But you *can't* mean Mr. *Tyco* Bass!" broke in Mrs. Topman.

"But we do, Mom — we climbed up the mountain to the Hall of the Ancient Ones, and he was there with Mebe and Oru — Ta's Wise Men, you remember — who had disappeared because they were so unhappy about what they'd done."

"And when we saw Mr. Bass there, he told us that after he left Basidium he was going to live in another solar system —"

"Now look, boys," interrupted Cap'n Tom, holding up a hand as though he wanted right this minute to get everything absolutely straight, "you can't mean Mr. *Tyco* Bass. He's — well, that is — he's gone, you remember. But Mr. Theo Bass —"

"No, no, *not* Mr. Theo Bass," cried Chuck. "Mr. Theo Bass decided to stay on Basidium, by the way, Grandpop. He says that's his home from now on,

175

and that he'd been searching all over the world for the place he belonged — and Basidium's it. No, we mean *our* Mr. Bass, you know — our special Mr. Bass."

"We got trapped in the Hall of the Ancient Ones, Cap'n Tom, because a boulder got dislodged and everything came crashing down and blocked the hall and we thought we were finished. But then Mr. Bass led us out through a secret passage he remembered from centuries ago. And then he vanished. He's gone away to another part of our galaxy to get on with his work. He says there are other solar systems out there."

Dr. and Mrs. Topman and Cap'n Tom all looked at one another.

"Gone to another——" began Cap'n Tom, but couldn't finish.

Dr. Topman cleared his throat.

"You know, boys," he said briskly and sensibly, "it seems to me that before we all sit down and hear about your adventures, you should really have a good sleep first. Look at Chuck — the boy's positively staggering with weariness."

"But why *would* he be?" protested David, wanting more than anything to have a big breakfast and tell everything right now. "We slept almost all the

176

way home." All the same, he thought, it was odd. Because he *did* feel kind of weak in the pins and light in the head, come to think of it.

But then, just as they were about to set off, something occurred to David. He turned, puzzled, toward Horatio, who had been peculiarly silent all this time. And there was Horatio, looking at them like a hound-dog with his old anxious, strained expression.

"I can't understand it," he exclaimed piteously. "I simply can't understand it. I cannot remember one thing of what you've been saying. All this you've been telling about — the Hall of the Ancient Ones, going up into the mountains, Mr. Bass's being there, and the mountain caving in — has faded, just faded away. Dimly I seem to recall certain scenes. But I can't remember how anything *looked!*" And here Horatio beat both fists against his forehead as though to *make* his poor muzzy mind do what was expected of it. "*Why* can't I remember? What's the matter with me? I feel — I feel as if my head were full of cotton wool. I only know that I've been to Basidium and seen wonderful things — things that most human beings would never believe; that *I* wouldn't believe if I hadn't seen them with my own eyes. But exactly what it looked like is drifting away — just . . . drifting away!"

Well, David exclaimed silently and feeling sorry for Horatio in spite of himself, you could look in that darned old notebook of yours. And then as if in answer to these unspoken words, Horatio suddenly snatched his precious notebook from his pocket and whipped it open.

"But it's all right," he cried. "Why do I keep forgetting that it's all here? Yes — this is what I wrote on the space ship *going* to Basidium before I fell asleep: all about the Stroboscopic Polarizing Filter that fellow Bass invented and which will enable us here on earth to see Basidium again. That filter must be recovered at once — for science — yes, that's the first thing to be done. I shall need it for my lecture. . . . And then — these are my plans for attacking the problem as a whole: all very clear and concise. Yes. And now, the notes I took *on* Basidium . . ." Here, with a te- s- frightened look, Horatio hesitated, licked his finger, laid it upon the next leaf — and turned.

Then the most awful thing happened. His hand, suspended in mid-air, began to tremble. His mouth, his pointed nose his sharp chin, his whole face, all seemed to loosen and sag as though they were melting, and it seemed as if Horatio Q. Peabody, the brilliant, alert, assured, triumphant Horatio, were actually about to burst into tears.

"Oh, no!" broke from him in low, hoarse tones. "No — no — no. . . ."

"Professor Peabody!" cried Mrs. Topman in alarm. "Why, what is the matter with you? Are you ill?"

But Horatio did not answer. Silently he flipped over one page after another. And then he began to shake his head — and he *kept* shaking his head as though he were suddenly an old, old man with the ague. At last the notebook fell from his nerveless hand.

"All gone," he whispered. "All gone. Hen-tracks — that's what it is, just hen-tracks."

Now Chuck darted over and picked up the book and opened it. Then he turned and held it out, his eyes wide with wonder.

"Sure," he breathed. "That's it. It's all in Basidiumite, of course. So now he can't read it. It's just scratchings, just gibberish. He can't remember the language, so now he can't remember how to read it. Poor old Horatio!"

"Oh, Professor Peabody," exclaimed Mrs. Topman in pity, going over to him and laying her hand on his shoulder, "never mind! You mustn't take it so hard. We really feel it's much better, after all, that the little Basidiumites go on living their lives all peaceful and undisturbed. Otherwise it's like upsetting the balance of nature — only disaster can follow. Now you just come on up to the house and have a nice breakfast, and then you'll feel ever so much more like yourself."

Horatio had sunk onto a rock, and now he lifted his head and looked at her out of haggard eyes.

"Madam," he said, and you could tell he was heartbroken, "if there is anything I do *not* want at this moment, it is a nice breakfast. I should be sick. There is only one thing I want and that is to decipher what I have written here." And he took his notebook from Chuck and replaced it in his jacket pocket. "I do not mind admitting to you that I have a fine mind — a *very* fine mind. And I intend to bend all its powers upon deciphering this language. The mystery of the Rosetta Stone was broken, and thus the translation of Egyptian hieroglyphs was given to the world. What man has done, I can do. Now please — I wish to be left alone."

And so they left him alone.

And when they looked back every now and then, there he still sat on the rock, quite motionless, his cheek resting on his palm, staring out in silent meditation over the sparkling, dancing, early morning blue of the calm Pacific.

CHAPTER 19

Horatio's Escape

Mrs. Topman said that the boys could both sleep in David's room and then have breakfast together later *if* they promised to go to sleep at once.

"But, Mom, what if we can't? We can't help it if we can't, can we?"

"No, David, you can't. But you will go to sleep if you will let yourselves. No whispering and laughing, now! Otherwise, back Chuck goes to his own house."

Well, it seemed to David he hadn't been asleep two minutes when his eyes flew open and he stared at the ceiling saying to himself quite distinctly, "What is Horatio Q. Peabody doing?"

He sat up. The clock by his bedside said 7:30, which meant he and Chuck had been asleep about an hour. He listened — not a sound. And when he got up on his knees and looked out of the window, it seemed as though the ocean must have come right up to lap against his window sill. For he couldn't see a thing. After the glorious early morning sun in which he and Chuck and Horatio had landed, the fog, as it very often does during the summer months along the Monterey peninsula, had come in thick and heavy. Grotesque, half-seen, were the trees, now faintly visible, now lost again in the wavering, winding fog. Drip, drip, drip went the drops of mist from rainpipe, bush, and branch. So thick was the drifting grayness that not even the chicken house or the garage could be seen. And even the falling of the waves on Cap'n Tom's beach sounded thick and muffled like hushed, slow breathing.

Now the other bed creaked and David turned and there was Chuck sitting up and blinking at him like a startled chipmunk with his hair pushed up into a crest.

"Hey," said Chuck in a low, urgent voice, "I've been worrying so hard in my sleep that I woke myself right up. We've got to get out of here and see what that Horatio Peabody's up to!"

"Just what I was thinking," said David. "Let's get going."

Without a word the two boys hurried into their

clothes and in another five minutes they were passing through the kitchen, where they spied a note propped up on the drainboard. It was from David's mother, and it said that if the boys awoke before she returned from getting breakfast for old Mrs. Gallagher, who was ill and alone, they were to eat their cereal and cook themselves some soft-boiled eggs. She would be back about 8:30 or 9. And they were to eat a large, *calm* breakfast, with no shenanigans at the table.

Silently David and Chuck looked at each other across the note. The rich smell of bacon still tantalized the air. The fragrance of hot buttered toast was just beginning to fade. Chuck swallowed longingly. Then he frowned.

"Let's go," he said sternly.

Outside, they hurried off close together, and not a glimpse of the world was visible beyond the small, perpetually advancing circle in which the boys moved down the cliff path toward the beach. All sounds were dulled. Someone was hammering far off, but it was as though the person hammered under a blanket.

Now they came to the rock on which they had left Horatio, but the rock was empty. Why should this seem ominous — this vacancy? It wouldn't be sensible to expect that Horatio would have remained sitting there during the past hour, with the fog coming in damp and penetrating and cold. Still — still, for some reason, David felt a sharp needle of worry urgently pricking him. On they went.

Now they were on the beach, but could only tell this to be the beach from the sand directly under their feet and the deep, long roll of breakers off to their right. All was hidden. *Hush-sh-sh*, went the sea.

But now suddenly Chuck put out his hand and grabbed David's arm.

"Listen!" he hissed.

Faintly, faintly, it seemed to David that he could hear the sounds of *busy-ness*. Yes, just that: little, quick, hurried sounds — the hard click of metal against metal, then a short, sharp scrape as if something were being hurriedly screwed together. It was as if someone were in a tremendous hurry to get something finished. And the sounds came from the direction of the cave!

They looked down as they ran forward, and now they saw the imprint of several pairs of feet — two sets going away from the cave, which would be Cap'n Tom's and Dr. Topman's, for they had rolled the space ship back into hiding, and then another set of prints going to the cave, which must be Horatio's. Already the shape of the future was gathering itself into an awful picture in David's head, yet he could not believe what he was beginning to think. There in the cave should be the hidden ship, together with those extra fuel tanks that Mr. Theo had stored for other trips to Basidium; but *would* they be there?

"Oh, no, Chuck — he can't do it — he can't!"

They stumbled forward, their eyes on the tracks that would lead them to the cave. And those busy, desperate, urgent sounds of preparation were becoming louder and more distinct. Yet now they seemed to come not from in front of them, but rather from the right, down towards the sea. The boys wavered, then by some common, unspoken consent, they ran on ahead till at last they came to the cave's mouth.

The cave was empty. And when they went inside it took only a glance to see that two of Mr. Theo's fuel containers were gone.

Now they turned and followed through the winding, drifting mist the two parallel tracks of the wheeled frame on which the space ship had been pushed down to the rock. And then — just as David touched Chuck's arm to point out to him the tall, spiring shape that loomed just ahead — faintly, imperceptibly, the mist began to glow with a soft, pinkish bronze light. At the same time it seemed to become thinner, more transparent; and in that weird illumination, as the sun tried to break through the fog, they saw Horatio. His back was to them, he was bent over, and with violent, almost savage movements he seemed to be tightening some reluctant bolt or screw. Above him towered the space ship, its whole length mistily gleaming a pale, silvery gold.

The boys halted — and stared at it. Never had they seen the ship so beautiful except on Basidium in the Mushroom Planet's eerie blue-green air. The fog drifted about the ship's smooth sides like rosy smoke, and David had the feeling, just for a moment, that it had already taken off into the skies.

Now Horatio straightened and glanced quickly, guiltily from side to side, and then for the first time David saw on the sand the empty fuel tanks which he had removed in order to install the new ones. Fiercely he threw down his tools and plunged his hands into his pockets as though searching for something. He exclaimed in a low, angry voice — then turned, and stared straight at them.

"Professor Peabody!" cried David, starting to-

ward him. "You can't go! You can't! It's too late! You'll be lost!" And he and Chuck sprang at Horatio and clutched that lean, writhing, twisting figure.

"Let me go — let me go," gasped Horatio. Then for a second the boys had him, flat on his back, and they could see how he was panting, his nostrils flared, his mouth open, his eyes wide and glazed and unseeing, like a trapped animal's. "I must go — you've got to let me go. I'm forgetting it all — the whole thing's almost gone!"

"You can't. You *can't* go —"

"All I can remember is that I went to a planet called Basidium and that I traveled through the skies — *50,000 miles through the skies!*" Now he struggled to be free with almost unbelievable strength. "I must go again — let me go —"

"But, Professor Peabody — remember the hole in space! It's up there, right in your path! Remember what Mr. Theo said: *You can only leave earth at a certain time because the path of the hole moves in an orbit.* Please don't go! Listen! *You've got to listen.*"

Suddenly Horatio lay deathly still. His whole body went limp and his eyes closed, and for a moment David thought they had hurt him. Perhaps he was unconscious. David stared up at Chuck (who had hold of Horatio's legs) in horror — and then like a snake Horatio gave one violent twist and threw the boys aside as if they had been chips of wood.

With a cry like a banshee's Horatio darted toward the rock, ran up it quick as a lizard, leaped into the ship, and leaned out grinning.

"Now you *shan't* stop me!" he cried with insane glee. "No one on earth shall stop me — and in two hours precisely I shall be on Basidium!" Then he wrenched the door closed and they could hear him bolt it tight.

In speechless horror the boys stared up at the window of the ship, and David felt himself shaking all over. Then the thin, triumphant face of Horatio Peabody appeared and he smiled an awful smile. *Get back! Get back!* he motioned to them, and immediately they turned and raced away.

Now there came a splitting, crackling roar, and for the third time Cap'n Tom's beach bore on its face the burned and blackened patch of sand which told of the take-off of the space ship for Basidium.

CHAPTER 20

The Return
to Space

As THOUGH the final, terrible act of a play had taken place and now the curtain had gone down, the fog once more closed in and the bronze glow, which had lighted it, faded.

Chuck and David remained motionless where they stood. The ship was gone as though it had never existed. Horatio was gone. Even now, with that look of wild triumph on his face, he was speeding through earth's atmosphere at 7 miles per second. Soon — in a moment or two — he would be far beyond it, and dashing headlong toward that whirling, downward-plunging force, that invisible maelstrom which had taken the swarm of meteors and sucked them into another dimension beyond all ken of man.

"We *tried* to save him, Chuck," whispered David.

"Mr. Bass tried to *tell* him, didn't he, Dave? He

said, 'If you go against the Laws, you will be brought to destruction.' "

Slowly the boys began the climb back across the beach toward home.

"But he wouldn't listen," went on David in a dazed voice. "He just wouldn't listen. He laughed at Mr. Bass. He defied him. He didn't care about anything, I guess, but just doing what *he* wanted to do. But, Chuck —" And now David stopped suddenly and he looked at Chuck as though cheered by some ray of hope. "Listen. Maybe, while he was sitting there on that rock, he figured out some way he could set the controls so that his vector would take him above or below the hole in space. He was smart —"

"But not that smart, Dave," intoned Chuck like a stolid Fate. "He said he'd be on Basidium in two hours exactly. That means he's using the same vector. Uh-uh. He's a goner — that's what Horatio Q. is."

The boys started forward again, each thinking his own thoughts, and then again David stopped and put a hand on Chuck's arm.

"Chuck, listen — remember what Mr. Theo said? He told us that if Horatio, by some slim chance, ever got back to Basidium, we were to watch two hours after the take-off, if we knew of it, and Mr. Theo would give a signal of three long flashes and a short one when the space ship landed. Then we'd know Horatio was there, and that he'd never, never leave Basidium again."

But Chuck's mouth drew downward and he shook his head slowly back and forth.

"Listen, Dave, if Horatio's so smart he can figure his way past the hole, then not even Mr. Theo could keep him from leaving if he wanted to get back to earth and start his plans for digging up Basidium. Boy, I'll feel sorry for the Basidiumites if *he* ever gets up there again. That Horatio — he'd just be . . . undefeatable! He wouldn't even *touch* the Drink of Forgetfulness a second time — he'd be too clever for that. No, Basidium's done for if he ever gets back again."

The boys stood on the beach in silence for a moment trying to determine the exact strength of Horatio's incredible will power. And just then it seemed to them that nothing — nothing in heaven or earth — could stop him from doing what he was determined to do. For it might well have been that, with his great store of astronomical knowledge, he had somehow figured a safe vector to Basidium.

Presently Chuck looked at his watch and his eyes narrowed.

"It was twenty-five minutes of eight when we left the house. Now it's eight. That means Horatio left at about five minutes of. Right?"

"Right! And so he'll land on Basidium at about five minutes of ten — *if he lands!*"

"Dave, let's watch. Let's go to Mr. Bass's and take turns watching Basidium, beginning about twenty minutes of ten. Then, if he lands, we'll catch the signal."

An hour and forty minutes later, the boys, their stomachs aching with hunger but with the pangs of hunger ignored, were to be seen crouched tensely at the eyepiece of Mr. Bass's telescope. The little gray-lighted observatory was silent. Not even the cheep of a bird was to be heard from the muffled stillness outside.

First Chuck watched, then David. The moments passed.

"Time, Chuck?"

"Ten of ten. He's got five minutes more. But, of course, Mr. Theo might not know right away."

"He'll know. He'll hear the space ship."

Slowly, slowly, the minute hand on Chuck's

watch crept toward the number eleven, while the little red second hand pushed round and round. At precisely five minutes of ten, it was David who was glued to the eyepiece.

Chuck's hand trembled on his shoulder, then its pressure sharpened.

"Let *me* look now! Let *me* look, Dave! You can't stick there forever!"

Reluctantly David moved away. Was he to miss the stupendous moment of Horatio Q. Peabody's historic and lonely landing on Basidium? Was he to miss the sight of those four flashes signaling across 50,000 miles of space?

But — no. For as the minutes ticked and ticked away, past five minutes of ten, past ten o'clock itself, no signal came. At five minutes after, David, whose turn it was, raised his head.

"Perhaps your watch is wrong, Chuck."

Wordlessly Chuck went over to Mr. Bass's desk and picked up the little traveling clock which Mr. Theo had left there. It said exactly five minutes after ten.

They watched for another half hour, and then David's eyes widened and the black pupils grew huge.

"Chuck, he's gone. He's missed his mark. Just think of it: *he's gone entirely!*"

But amazingly enough, Chuck laughed aloud.

"Dave!" he cried. "Remember the limerick about the young lady named Bright? When you travel slower than the speed of light, as we do on earth, you go forward in time and get old. If we were to travel faster than that, like the lady named Bright, we'd get younger. But if anyone were to travel at *just* that speed, as Horatio's doing now on the other side of the hole, he'd stay *just exactly the same* as he was at the second he plunged in! And remember how happy and triumphant he looked at the window of the space ship when he took off?"

"Ye-e-e-s," breathed David, the whole thing beginning to dawn on him at last. "I see, Chuck — I get it. There he is, in that other dimension, just exactly as he was when he left our universe."

The boys looked at one another, their faces lighted with amazement. And between them hung the astounding picture of Horatio Q. Peabody, alert, erect, beaming with eager anticipation, speeding through infinities of time, caught in one moment forever — and forever tilted on the invisible edge of attaining what he longed for most — the return to Basidium!

CHAPTER 21

Pride Goeth . . .

A MONTH PASSED.

And sometimes David would wake in the middle of the night and it would come over him afresh: how even now, at this very moment, Horatio was existing somewhere in an absolutely unthinkable state, quite unable ever to get out of it. Or maybe the two boys would be walking along the street together, or sitting up in Mr. Bass's observatory in the evening, looking at the moon through the telescope, or watching Basidium, and David would be struck all over again by Horatio's plight.

On such an evening, he said:

"Gee, poor old Horatio, he makes me sad."

"Well, but what the heck, Dave, he had it coming to him. Who was he, anyway, to want to change everything no matter what happened to anybody else?"

196

"Yes, but Chuck, to get caught like that and to have to just go on — and on — and on . . ."

"With the same expression on his face the whole darned time!" Chuck murmured, and shuddered, as if this thought, of them all, were too much to bear.

They said nothing, each boy lost in imagining, until once more, quite idly, Chuck leaned forward, put an eye to the telescope . . . and let out a yelp of amazement.

"Dave! Dave! Look! It's the signal! It's happened! Mr. Theo's signaling — look!"

David leaped up, knocked over his stool, fell on Chuck, shoved him out of the way, and banged his face on the telescope. But he had no idea what he was doing.

"Yes — so it is," he whispered, staring upward and clutching the telescope so hard his knuckles turned white. "It's the signal — three long flashes and a short — three long flashes and a short — 50,000 miles away!" Now it was David's turn to be knocked aside.

"Let me look — let me see again! Yes, there it is, Dave! It's the signal. My golly, what's happening? Has Horatio *landed?* He *must* have! *Now* what's he going to do? Oh, gee, the poor little Mushroom People!"

At last the signaling stopped. The boys kept watch for a little longer but nothing happened. Basidium remained as it had been before: pale blue-green and peaceful, a tiny jewel suspended in space.

"But, Chuck, I don't get it. A whole month has passed since Horatio took off. Surely he couldn't have —"

"Yes, but, Dave — remember — in space there's no time — that is, for Horatio there's no time. It's all just one big long NOW. So maybe he got out of the hole in some way. But how could he get from there to Basidium?"

"I don't get it, Chuck. I just don't get it. But surely Mr. Theo's signal means *something*." He was silent, then suddenly he jumped up. "I don't know why, but I have a feeling we ought to get going. Hurry — maybe we'll be too late — I don't know for what, but I just have this feeling. Remember what Mr. Theo said? That he'd signal, too, if anything unusual happened, or were about to happen."

David was across the little room in a flash and clattering down the steep, narrow stairs almost before Chuck could catch his breath or take in what David had said.

"But, listen," he yelled, stumbling after David

and racing to the front door and slamming it behind him, "listen, we ought to get going *where?* Where're we going, Dave?"

"To the ocean," David called back, racing along the shadowy street that led toward his own house and Cap'n Tom's beach.

"But *why* the ocean?" persisted Chuck, and then finally managed to catch up. "Why the ocean, Dave? What's the matter with you? Have you gone crazy?"

"Nope," returned David, running fast. "And I don't know why the ocean. But I've got this feeling. I had it so strong up at Mr. Bass's, I just had to get going. You go on home if you like."

"*Home!*" Chuck snorted. "Me — go *home?* After Mr. Theo's *s*ignal? Boy, you *are* crazy!"

The moon was huge, still low on the horizon as though it had just climbed up out of the sea, and in front of it, along a broad path, the waves ran glittering. The sand of the beach was all silver, the faces of the rocks turned to the moon were silver, and all the big rumbling rollers had silver backs that curved over, smooth and powerful.

Chuck and David stood at the wave-line where a lip of foam scalloped the sand. Without speaking they looked out over the water at the moon and sometimes David would stare up overhead as though expecting something. At their backs a small wind sighed in the cypress trees.

In a moment or two, David grasped Chuck by the arm and silently pointed upward at the dark sky. Chuck's eyes followed the pointing finger.

"*What is it*, Dave?" But David did not answer, only stood with his head back, watching. "Is it a falling star?"

Whatever it was, descending swiftly on some invisible path that must surely end in the ocean in front of them, it gleamed indeed like some falling star. But it was not a star. David heard Chuck's breath draw in sharply, for now a strange, high whistling assailed their ears out of the night sky, a whistling that grew and grew in almost painful intensity. Nearer it came, and nearer, until at last, for the flick of an instant, the shining object, whatever it was, flashed across their sight in the full light of the moon — and then was gone — plunging into the sea before their very eyes just at the moment when the high, well-nigh unendurable whine had reached its highest and most piercing note.

Now silence closed in. The sea was smooth and quiet, the broad path of the moon glinted as before, and the face on the moon seemed to have seen nothing unusual. But Chuck turned and looked at David. His eyes were enormous.

"It was our ship, Dave. *That was our space ship! I saw it!* I knew before it came down, and then when it was almost down, right over the ocean — I saw it. *I know it was our ship!*"

"Chuck, it'll come back to the surface. Maybe, somehow, we can get it. C'mon!"

As though they were possessed, they ran down to where the great rocks bordered the sea and carried the shore out into deep water. They ran up over the face of the rocks, down into deep, black gullies, and up again into the moonlight, panting in their impatient eagerness to get high on top. At last they looked down over the whole ocean stretched beneath them.

"See anything, Dave?" Chuck was squinting, straining his eyes to catch sight of their ship bobbing around somewhere out there on the swiftly running surface of the sea. But David only shook his head. Again and again they turned in a slow semicircle from left to right in the hope of catching some fleck of moving silver in their vision. But nothing was to be seen — or was the fleck of silver lost in the glittering waves, so that moonlight was not to be told from the floating body of their ship?

201

"It's hopeless, Chuck. What a couple of fools we are to think we can spot something like that at night. Only I thought that if . . ."

"If we *could* spot it," finished Chuck sadly, "we could keep it from maybe crashing on the rocks and being smashed to pieces like our other ship."

"But it's no use. We'll have to wait till morning."

"And the tide's coming in. So if the ship *does* come with it, it just *might* be washed safely ashore."

"Unless she comes in opposite here — opposite these rocks —"

"And in that case —" But Chuck's voice hung suspended in mid-air. "*Listen!*"

David listened. The night wind rustled past their ears. The waves crashed on the rocks. But between one crash and another he heard something.

"Help! Help!" The tiny voice came faintly. "Help!"

"*Horatio!*"

"But it — it *can't* be!"

"*H-e-l-p!*"

Madly leaping from one cliff to the next, rolling, sliding on the seats of their pants, falling into rock pools until they were soaked to the knees, Chuck and David scrambled down to where the waves were

202

roaring in, forgetting danger entirely in their frenzy to find Horatio. Now they came right to the edge of the rocks above the foaming water, where surely the next wave would crash down and cover them. The sea heaved itself — the thundering whiteness came in.

"Watch *out*, Dave! Watch o-u-t!"

They ran, but when they looked back over their shoulders after the wave had receded, they saw something dark lying on the smooth sand of the little inlet below them.

It moved. Weakly it lifted an arm. It gathered itself. It . . .

"*It's Horatio!*" screamed Chuck.

David on one side, Chuck on the other, they heaved up that poor gasping, shivering, waterlogged remnant of humanity.

"What happened?" it got out faintly. "Where — where am I?"

"Now, now, Horatio, just take it easy. You've come a long way —"

"We'll get you home —"

"Just sit here for a minute till you pull yourself together, then we'll help you up the hill."

"Can you, Horatio? You'd better get home; you might catch cold."

Horatio staggered to his feet and stared all about as though he could scarcely believe his eyes. Then he seemed to chirk up. Impatiently he loosed himself from the boys' sustaining hands.

"I don't *want* to sit down," he said in his old sharp, abrupt fashion. "I'm all right. Perfectly all right. Bit wet — but that's to be expected after a swim in one's clothes. But why is it night? That's the only thing I can't figure. *Why is it night?*"

David swallowed. He gazed at Horatio, then at Chuck, and Chuck seemed too astounded by all this to speak.

"Horatio, listen to me," begged David. "You've been through an awful experience. You must be calm. Have you any idea what's happened to you?"

Horatio frowned slightly and seemed to reflect.

"Well," he replied, "let me see now. The last thing I remember is sitting on that rock over there. Seems to me your mother was trying to persuade me to do something I didn't want to do. But *what?* And I was unhappy, terribly unhappy. But why? I know I gave my lecture. And it was a great success. It was, wasn't it?" Horatio suddenly interrupted himself anxiously. Then he recovered. "Yes, I remember it was. Wait'll Dr. Frobisher hears about *that! He's* not the only one who can give lectures. Well, anyway, so then I must have gone for a walk — climbed up over those rocks, maybe, right to the top, and then — fallen in." Now Horatio's voice stopped and a peculiar look came over his face. "Yes, but I think I must have gone to sleep up there first, because I seem to remember a dream — really a horrible dream. But it's all so vague . . ." Again his voice petered out and for a moment the boys could see that his face held a look that was quite terror-stricken.

"Do go on, Horatio. What was the dream?" Chuck pressed him.

"Or wouldn't you rather go up to the house and get dry and then tell us?" asked David.

"No, no. Let me think. I seem to remember a fight. Some sort of fight on the beach, and I won. But even so, I — I — well, then, after a long while I remember something terrible, as though I were being wrenched bone from bone. It was so awful I can't begin to describe it. . . ."

That must have been when he went through the hole in space, thought David. That was the experience of going from one dimension to another.

"And all the while it seems to me I was grinning, for some insane reason, but I can't think why. Grinning all the time, I was, and I kept saying over and over to myself, without stopping, the words, 'This is forever — this is forever — and forever — and forever — and forever. . . .' Oh, it was frightful — I can't begin to tell you! But I *wasn't* crazy, not for a moment. *I knew.*" Suddenly Horatio put his head in his hands, and Chuck and David stared at one another, appalled, over poor Horatio's bowed back, and then he straightened again "I had the feeling in my dream that this had something to do with pride — or vanity. But I can't think why. And then the awful thing happened again — the Jolt. But I can't really remember what it was all about — nor why I found myself in the ocean. But I did. So I must have fallen from the cliffs — and then started swimming. But it's all so strange — I don't understand — I don't understand at all."

"But you're safe now, Horatio," comforted Chuck. "It's all over and you're safe. And you'd better come along home with us and get into dry clothes. I think Dr. Topman's trousers would fit you better than my Gramp's. He's kind of tubby."

"Yes," said Horatio, beginning to move slowly across the sand. "Yes, boy, you're quite right. I'd better be getting home. *Home!* Good heavens —"

and all at once Horatio seemed positively galvanized into action. "I've simply *got* to get the night train out of here. Do you realize I have the whole of Dr. Frobisher's manuscript to prepare for the publishers as well as the research for his next lecture? Hurry now! I haven't a moment to lose. What if he should have got back in my absence? But what am I thinking — I've only been gone two days. All the same, I *must* be there. You see, I am quite indispensable to him — as a matter of fact, it is really I who — I — who —" And then Horatio stopped. He stared down at the sand, and then looked up sideways.

What could he be thinking? wondered David. And what on earth will he say, what will he do, when he finds he has been gone, not two days, but almost *a whole month?*

"What, Horatio? It is you who *what?*" insisted Chuck.

"Good heavens, now why should that stupid old saying have come into my head? You know, the one about pride." And — would you believe it? — Horatio actually smiled, a kind of shamefaced, sheepish smile.

"You mean, 'Pride goeth before a fall,' Horatio?" asked Chuck.

"Oh, but you needn't worry about that now," said David. "You've *had* your fall!"

"Yes," agreed Horatio, taking a last look at the cliff before he turned to go on up the beach. "All the way from the top of those rocks. It's a wonder I wasn't killed."

He went on — stopped — and now a most amazing thing happened. For Horatio suddenly slapped a hand over his jacket pocket, looked puzzled, and then slowly pulled forth a swollen, sodden mass and stared at it in wonderment.

"What on earth . . . !" he exclaimed, and then with a gesture of extreme distaste, he flung the mass down and kicked it to one side into a rock pool. "Can't imagine," he muttered, while the boys stood staring first at Horatio, then at what had once been the pride, the passion, the very core and necessity of Horatio's existence — his precious notebook.

But now an even more astonishing thing happened. Again he felt his jacket, again looked puzzled, and this time drew forth a handful of stones (they might have been colored by daylight, but by moonlight they seemed only gray and black and white), which he slowly turned over, one by one, meanwhile shaking his head. "What litter one picks up and carries about with one. Can't even remember where —" But he did not finish. He simply tossed the stones away and walked on.

For a moment David stood where he was, watching, while a wave far out reared up its white back and came plunging in toward where the notebook lay and, not far off, the stones. The notebook would be picked up by the wave and never seen again. The stones would be buried in the sand, or in an hour or two be washed away and lost forever. But what if — thought David — what if in that notebook there lay some unimaginable key to the language of Basidium? Who could tell — who could tell? As for the stones, David could not bear that even one pebble of the Mushroom Planet should be lost — and in a moment he had recovered both the notebook and the jewels of Basidium before the wave could reach them, and had stuffed them into his pocket so that Horatio should not see them.

"Yes," Horatio was saying to Chuck as David caught up, "yes, I might have been killed. Some fall! In fact, I should say that a fall like that ought to do me for the rest of my life, don't you think?"

"Pre-*cise*ly!" came a high, airy, far-off voice, so high and airy and far-off that there could be no doubt as to its owner.

But when David turned eagerly to look, there was no one there.

Take another ride to the Mushroom
Planet in . . .
*The Wonderful Flight to the
Mushroom Planet*

One night after dinner when David was reading *Doctor Dolittle in the Moon,* and his father
was reading the newspaper, and his mother was
darning socks, his father suddenly exclaimed:

"Well, now, *that's* very odd!"

"What's odd?" David and his mother both
asked at once.

"Why," said his father, "this notice in the paper."

David went over to look, and there, down at
the very bottom corner of the next to the last
page of the newspaper, were a few lines of print.
But though the rest of the newspaper was
printed in black, this little notice was in green.
Here is what it said:

WANTED: A small space ship about eight
feet long, built by a boy, or by two boys, between the ages of eight and eleven. The

ship should be sturdy and well made, and should be of materials found at hand. Nothing need be bought. No adult should be consulted as to its plan or method of construction. An adventure and a chance to do a good deed await the boys who build the best space ship. Please bring your ship *as soon as possible* to Mr. Tyco M. Bass, 5 Thallo Street, Pacific Grove, California.

Well, a notice like that sprung suddenly on any boy, just because of its general air of mystery and urgency, would be enough to start him simmering. But for David it was stupendous!

The sight of that little green notice in the paper set him vibrating like a harp in the wind. *Build a real space ship all his own.* Why, he'd never thought of that! And yet, why not? And then, after that —

"But it's a joke," said Dr. Topman firmly, after a moment or two in which he must have been cogitating. "I'll bet you anything it's just some sort of joke — and a pretty poor one at that."

"Oh, but Father, it can't be! *Why* would it be a joke?"

But Dr. Topman only muttered to himself

something about its being a crime to lead children on like that, and about there being a catch to it somewhere.

David looked at his mother. She winked at him and held out her scissors, and in a minute David had the notice all cut out and neatly folded up in his pocket.

Tomorrow morning, he said to himself, he'd begin working on his design for the ship — or he'd begin hunting around to see how much material he could find to build it. And maybe Chuck Masterson could dig out a lot of old boards and stuff nobody wanted any more over in his grandfather's boathouse. But then all at once he thought: Why not begin drawing the plans right away? So he got some paper and a pencil and started to work.

"Father!" exclaimed David as he drew his first lines.

"Yes, David," answered his father patiently, putting down his newspaper.

"What would the earth look like from way out in the sky, thousands of miles away?"

"We-e-ll," replied Dr. Topman, seeming to consider, "I can't imagine. But one thing I know, all around us stretches the absolute black of space, even with the sun burning and flaming away out there like a huge furnace — space that is almost empty inside and around our solar system, but that beyond is crowded with stars even in the daytime. Because, as a matter of fact, you see, there *is* no daytime out there — no wind, no sound, nothing but blackness and the eternal movements of those little points of light."

No daytime, no wind, no sound, nothing but blackness!

"But Father, *why* is there no daytime there, even if the sun is shining?"

"Because there is nothing out there to *reflect* the sun's light, David. Atmosphere, made up of gases, surrounds our earth, so that whatever part of the earth the sun is shining on has light — the atmosphere reflects it. The atmosphere carries sound, causes the winds. But not out in space. And if you were thousands of miles away and looking at the earth," continued Dr. Topman, "you would see both day and night from there at once, if the sun were in the right position."

By bedtime, half an hour later, David had a most beautiful diagram of his space ship all finished.

The ship was long and smooth and cigar-shaped, with a slender pointed nose. It had one big window at the front. Just back of the window there was a door which could be bolted tight. The ship had no wings, but it had four broad blades for a tail, set at right angles to one another around the rocket exhaust. They were level at the ends so that the space ship could sit upended on them quite firmly, and they were curved on the inside edges where they extended below the exhaust. There was a cross-section drawing of the ship, so that you could see its interior, and a rear-view, a side-view, and a front-view drawing.

Tomorrow was Tuesday, the second day of Easter vacation. He and Chuck would have to work fast. They would have to keep their plans secret, and the building of the space ship hidden — maybe down in that cave on Cap'n Tom's beach — so no other fellows could see what they were doing and steal their ideas. And they wouldn't even tell Cap'n Tom, who was Chuck's grandpop, because Cap'n Tom would want to help build.

Now David wandered away to his own room and slowly and thoughtfully began to get undressed. Finally, quite a bit later, and still thinking hard about frameworks and air pressure and velocity and all that, he climbed into bed and curled into a ball. But when his father and mother came in to say good night and turn out the light, he sat up again.

"You know what?" he said, looking up at the moon that was sending a pale beam through his window.

"What, David?" asked his father and mother, stopping to listen.

"I'd like to find a little planet just my size — not a big one like the earth that takes months and months to get around, but a nice *little* one that you could explore in a day or two."

"But I'm afraid that's not possible, David," said Dr. Topman, smiling down at him, "not for ten or twenty years yet, or maybe even fifty. Might be something to look forward to, though."

"Perhaps you'll find it in your dreams, David," said his mother hopefully.

"But I don't *want* to find it in my dreams," said David impatiently. "That wouldn't do at all. I don't *want* it to be a dream. I want it to be *real!*"

Don't forget to read *The Wonderful Flight to the Mushroom Planet!*